Wake Up Little Susie

*Also by Ed Gorman
in Large Print:*

The Day the Music Died
Night Kills

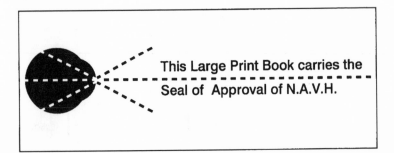

This Large Print Book carries the
Seal of Approval of N.A.V.H.

Wake Up Little Susie

Ed Gorman

Thorndike Press • Thorndike, Maine

Published in 2000 by arrangement with Carroll & Graf Publishers, Inc.

Thorndike Press Large Print Mystery Series.

The tree indicium is a trademark of Thorndike Press.

The text of this Large Print edition is unabridged.
Other aspects of the book may vary from the original edition.

Set in 16 pt. Plantin.

Printed in the United States on permanent paper.

Library of Congress Cataloging-in-Publication Data

Gorman, Edward.
    Wake up little Susie : a mystery / Ed Gorman.
      p. cm.
    ISBN 0-7862-2464-9 (lg. print : hc : alk. paper)
    1. Private investigators — Fiction. 2. Edsel automobile — Fiction. 3. Iowa — Fiction. 4. Large type books. I. Title.

PS3557.O759 W35 2000
813´.54—dc21
                                        00-025975

In memory of Dr. William R. Finn

The author would like to thank
Larry Segriff for his indispensable
help with this book.

Readers of *The Day the Music Died*
will note that this novel is set
a year previous.

"There's not much to see in a small town, but what you hear makes up for it."

— August Derleth

"There was the truth of virginity and the truth of passion, the truth of wealth and of poverty, of thrift and of profligacy, of carelessness and abandon. Hundreds and hundreds were the truths and they were all beautiful."

— Sherwood Anderson,
Winesburg, Ohio

PART I

One

So Elvis leaned over to me and said, "You know what it looks like?"

"What what looks like?"

"That grille."

"No," I said. "What's it look like?"

He grinned. "It looks just like a woman's —" He whispered a word naming the most private part of a woman's anatomy.

He wasn't really Elvis, of course.

On this Saturday, September 14, 1957, in Black River Falls, Iowa, on the lot of Keys Ford-Lincoln, there were at least a dozen Elvises, maybe eight James Deans, six Marlon Brandos, and maybe as many as twenty Kim Novaks. Everybody had to be somebody, so why not be somebody famous?

I suppose it's kind of sad, feeling that you need to be somebody else. For a long time I wanted to be Robert Ryan. I really like that crazed Irish intensity of his. But he didn't wear anything distinctive — like Elvis's hair or James Dean's red jacket or Marlon's rolled-up T-shirt — so even when I walked down the street pretending to be him, nobody knew. It was real frustrating. Maybe

Ryan will start wearing an eye patch.

Being something of a car aficionado, I had been waiting for this day for months. This was the day that the Ford family of Detroit, Michigan, would bestow upon us the most futuristic, the most exciting of all family automobiles, the Edsel.

I guess it's kind of funny how we look at cars. I remember this Russian diplomat saying that Americans were the only people he knew who wrote pop songs about their cars. Heck, I did even better than that. I *dreamed* about cars. Oh, sure, I dreamed about girls, especially the beautiful Pamela Forrest, but I also dreamed about cars. About owning, in addition to my red Ford ragtop, a black chopped and channeled '49 Merc. Or one of those little red street rods.

I even had a couple of dreams about the Edsel, and what it would look like would be downright fantastic. . . .

According to *Time* magazine, Ford had spent $10 million advertising this launch. Even poet Marianne Moore had been asked to help name the vehicle. Her choice had been the "Moongoose." Declining her suggestion was about the only smart thing Ford had done in bringing this car to market.

Keys Ford-Lincoln was so crowded, they'd had to hire extra cops to direct traffic.

An hour before the unveiling, right on the same concrete slab where the cloth-covered Edsel would be brought, there had been a talent show. All the expected acts appeared — baton twirlers, tap-dancing twins, pig-call masters, Elvis impersonators, Lawrence Welk imitators, baggy-pants drunk acts, and two (God love 'em) little girls wearing spangly top hats who sang "God Bless America" with tears in their eyes — but the one I liked best was the saw player who kept cutting himself on the teeth of his instrument. By the time he'd finished "Ebb Tide" he was badly in need of medical attention.

There was the high school marching band. There was a speech by the mayor. There were pennants and three dozen Brownies with hula hoops and two dozen Cub Scouts in Davy Crockett coonskin caps and twenty-three college boys trying to stuff themselves into a single phone booth.

And then there were all the Elvises.

Not only wasn't the guy next to me really Elvis, his opinion wasn't even original. A number of other men had expressed the same thing earlier in the day. About what the Edsel grille looked like, I mean.

And that was about the only good feature on the whole car. The rest of it looked like something out of a cartoon. *Piss elegant* was the proper term. It had gadgets previously unseen in automobiles; it had pastel colors heretofore unknown to automotive metal.

This wasn't just my reaction.

You could see it on virtually every face. It was like opening a birthday box to find a rat crawling around inside.

Being small-town folk the way we are, we didn't say any of this to Dick Keys, of course. The usually cool Dick Keys looked nervous. His story was that as the handsomest kid, not only in his class but in the entire valley, he would go on to marry his own kind: a beauty. Instead, he married a plain stout girl who just happened to be the *wealthiest* girl in the valley. There was no smoother salesman than Dick Keys, and he ran the Ford-Mercury dealership well day-to-day. But it was rumored, and I believe true, that his wife, who'd put up the money for the dealership, made most of the important decisions. Today, Dick wore a white button-down shirt, red-and-blue regimental-striped tie, and a pair of blue slacks. He was good-looking in the sort of way that the second lead in romantic comedies is good-looking. He never gets the girl. Dick's graying hair lent him an air of earnestness, and his slightly loose midsection reminded the rest of us mortals that when we reached Dick's age — he was in his early fifties — we too would be faded by time. If it could happen to Dick Keys, it could happen to any of us.

Dick was one of hundreds of Ford dealers who were just now realizing that Edsel Ford and Robert McNamara had stuck him with one hilariously ugly sonofabitch of a car.

Elvis snapped his collar up a little higher, gave me a lurid wink, cracked his gum, and said, "I gotta find me some chicks, man."

I got a hot dog and went over to where Keys had set up a little carnival: a small Ferris wheel, a few battered bumper cars, a pony ride, and some clowns who vaguely scared me the way clowns had always vaguely frightened me.

Keys had also rented some green park benches that pigeons had been decorating. I sat down on one and ate my dog.

I was just finishing up my lunch when I saw her, and it was a good thing I was almost done because my stomach did its usual flip-flop. The same kind of flip-flop it had been doing since that first day of fourth grade when I'd instantly fallen in love with her: the beautiful Pamela Forrest.

I once asked my mom if our family had ever been hexed. You know, if somebody had a grudge against Mom and Dad and put a curse on their firstborn, which would be

15

me. Condemn him to love a girl forever beyond his reach. I am twenty-three, a lawyer,
and have what they call "prospects." And I
have a '51 red Ford convertible with the
custom skirts, the louvered hood, and the
special weave top that most of the guys
around here, even the cool ones, envy.

That's my story. Hers is, she's been in love
with Stu Grant since ninth grade, just the
way I've been in love with her. He's big,
good-looking, rich, and powerful. He's also
married. Pamela's convinced he'll someday
leave his wife and take his rightful place at
her side. Right, just like Liz Taylor and
Eddie Fisher'll break up someday too.

She was licking an ice-cream cone. She
wore a crisp pink blouse and pink pedal
pushers and pink flats. The blouse and
pedal pushers had cute little black and
white poodles on them. Her golden hair
touched her shoulders, and her blue eyes
looked fresh and bright. Everybody says she
looks like Grace Kelly, and that's the neat
thing: she does but she doesn't *try* to. It
comes naturally for her. Just the way it does
for Grace Kelly. If you see my point.

"Hi, McCain."

"Hi."

"May I sit down?"

"Nah."

She looked startled. She's used to me making a fool of myself around her, so when I do otherwise it shakes her faith in how the universe works. "No?"

I grinned. "Sure."

"Oh, gosh, you scared me there, McCain."

We come from the area of town known as the Knolls, Pamela and I. Worst section in all of Black River Falls. Her grandfather had money till the Depression, which was when they'd been banished from mansion to Knolls. Pamela was raised to believe she was an exiled princess. Someday she'd have money again and would therefore be restored to the throne.

"What d' you think of the Edsel?" she asked between licks.

"What d' *you* think?"

"I asked you first."

"I think it's terrible."

"Me too. But I saw the Judge a few minutes ago and she loves it."

The judge she referred to is one Esme Anne Whitney. Before the big war (as distinct from the little one in Korea), the Whitneys owned this town. The city council, the police and fire departments, the newspaper, the school board, the Presbyterian church, and both banks were run by them. Then a yahoo family one generation up from the South — Sykes by name — got lucky working for the army during the big war building airstrips and took over much of what the Whitneys had controlled. Now there was a pitched battle between the two camps. Because my law practice couldn't support me, I used the private investigator's license I picked up after graduating from the University of Iowa law school to work for Judge Whitney. If Pamela labored under the delusion that she would someday be a princess, Judge Whitney labored under the delusion that she would someday reclaim the town from the barbaric hordes that had stolen it from her family. She saw virtually all citizens of Black River Falls as unclean, uncouth, uneducated, unappreciative, ungodly, and just about every other *un* you care to name. It was her often stated wish that the Whitneys would once again reign supreme so the "little people" would have the Whitneys to imitate and aspire to. The beautiful, elegant Pamela Forrest was her secretary.

"She loves it," I said, "because she used to date one of the Ford boys when she was at Smith and he was at Dartmouth. You know how she thinks. The upper classes have to stick together. Otherwise all of us Woolworth vulgarians'll overrun them."

"She's a lot nicer than you think."

"Yeah? When?"

"You should see her on Christmas Eve. Handing out those dimes to little poor kids."

"Yeah, that probably puts a real strain on her five-million-dollar bank account."

"She makes sure they're shiny and new, McCain. She's a stickler for that."

"She makes sure *what's* shiny and new?"

"The dimes."

"Ah."

"She goes to the bank and personally picks out every one."

"I'd call her a saint," I said, "if she didn't hate Catholics so much."

And that's when Pamela's stomach did a flip-flop. Or at least I imagined it did.

A silent Dreamboat Alert had sounded. That's what some of the teenage girls at the Rexall soda fountain counter call it when a cool guy comes into the drugstore.

This particular dreamboat was none other than Pamela's lifelong love, Stu Grant. And he was sans wife today, a fact that Pamela had no doubt noted instantly.

"Oh, gosh," she said, as if Tab Hunter had just appeared. She handed me her cone. "Here. Finish this for me, will you?"

She pushed the cone at me before I could say no. Being her slave, I took it. She went to work on herself, using the tools inside the small pink purse slung over her small pink shoulder. She touched up every inch of her lovely face and then jumped up and said, "See you, McCain."

Yes, I had been cursed. My dad or mom *had* to have done something to somebody with supernatural powers. Because I just kept right on loving her. No matter what she did to me. No matter how hopeless it was.

After I finished off her ice-cream cone, faintly tasting lipstick on its rim, I just sat and watched and felt good about living here. Most of the people I graduated law school with rushed off to big cities, mostly Chicago, which is only four and a half hours away. I'd spent four recent days there at a law conference Judge Whitney had sent me to, and now I was happily back home. For all its flaws, I love the place.

As if to confirm my regard for the town, Henry chose now to jump up on the bench. With his jaunty sailor's cap and his bow tie, Henry was looking his best. Henry is a duck, and as far as I know he's been a duck most of his life, though sometimes you have to wonder, the very human things he does.

Maybe he started out as a kid and evolved into a duck. Henry belongs to a farmer who plants corn west of town. He brings Henry in for special occasions, like Edsel Day.

Henry sat next to me and we watched the human parade roll past, the way it's been rolling past since those French trappers of three hundred years ago came down the Mississippi.

In their quiet way, the people here are fascinating, and Henry must agree because he sure was looking them over. There, for instance, was the Kennard family: quadruplets. Mother and father run ragged by them but proud all the same. There's Denny Farnham. Lost both legs in Korea but came back here and opened up his own service garage. He takes care of my Ford for me, and it's damned good care. There's Mike Braly. He runs a little flower shop and a lot of people whisper he's a queer because he's forty-two and never been married and always goes to Cedar Rapids or Iowa City on weekends — meeting other queers, is what some say. But he's a good guy and just about everybody likes him. And then there's Tom Holmes. When he was a senior in high school here he ran back an interception forty-eight yards to take us to State. The one and only time we'd ever been to State. It was a real accomplishment for a town of 25,000-plus, and even though it happened in '46, folks still treat him like a hero. I don't care much for sports but I respect Tom. His two older brothers were killed in Italy and his dad lost a leg on the railroad where he'd worked as a brakeman, and yet despite those bad breaks Tom turned out to be a prosperous land speculator. And there was Mel Sager, full-blooded Mesquakie, a guitar player who has appeared with Western stars like Marty Robbins and Webb Pierce and Jim Reeves, who comes back to see his mom and his sister three–four times a year. And then there were the high school girls. We seem to get a bumper crop every year. Not just good-looking but smart too, going off to Iowa City or Des Moines or Cedar Rapids or Omaha to become nurses and bookkeepers and legal secretaries, many of them — between you and me — probably a lot smarter than the men they work for.

Old folks needing relief from the hot sun, little kids needing bathrooms, sweet-faced junior high school girls needing attention from boys — a whole wonderful mix of people on this soft warm Indian-summer afternoon wandered around looking at the Edsels. Nice, easygoing, decent folks. I've got nothing against Chicago, but this is my home.

Car premieres are big deals in towns like ours. They're like opening nights. The big semis loaded with new cars roll in, and half the people in town start driving past the dealership for a glimpse. The cars are always covered up so you can only guess at how cool they look. Some of the semis come in late at night like they're carrying military cargo the Russians might try and hijack. The dealers are smart enough to stage the premieres so there's never a conflict. Chevy usually goes first, then Ford, then Chrysler, then the lesser lines: American Motors and, lately, Volkswagen.

"Hello, Sam."

I'd seen her walking toward me: Mrs. Irene Keys. Hers was a kind of sadly biblical story. The rich girl with the plain face who was just naturally a target for girls and boys alike who wanted to bask in the rarefied air of that wealth. She learned early how to dress well. As she got older, her plain features had taken on a handsomeness not unlike a piece of Roman sculpture. There was great character in her face now. And she learned early to be friendly and seemingly open, though you sensed a ferocious intelligence she tried to hide. Wealth *and* superior intelligence would have been too much for most folks to handle. Even the Judge had remarked on how impressive having lunch was with Mrs. Keys. "She's up on everything, McCain. You just don't expect to find that in a hick town like this one." Over the years, Mrs. Keys had several times asked me to visit her book club for a discussion. I guess because of my age, she thought I'd be able to explain the allure of Kerouac and Ginsberg and Corso and Ferlinghetti to small-town matrons.

Today, she wore a tailored brown suit that nearly matched the hennaed rinse she'd had put in her hair. She carried a shopping bag with KEYS LINCOLN on its side.

"Enjoying yourself, Sam?"

"Very much."

"Dick hasn't slept well for nearly a month, he's been so worried about the Edsel."

I lied. "Well, from the things I hear, everybody sure seems to like it."

"Really? When I see people, they give me very evasive answers."

I grinned. "They probably don't want to embarrass you with too much flattery."

She laughed. "Always ready to turn a bad moment aside with a good line, Sam. That's why it's so much fun having you around.

Any chance I could get you to come to the book club discussion we're having next month?"

"Who're you reading?"

"Henry Miller."

I thought of all the words old Henry put in his books. "Really?"

"Yes. And a couple of us have found words we — we aren't exactly sure what they mean. We *think* we know but we're not sure."

"The minister's wife going to be there again?"

She smiled. "She's the one who suggested it."

"Well, why not? Just as long as Cliffie doesn't bust us for possession of pornography."

"I'll make sure Dick puts the fix in. Isn't that what they call it when you bribe a policeman? A fix?"

"That's what you call it. And may I suggest, with Cliffie, that you bribe him with comics. He's big on the Green Hornet."

"I'll remind you later," she said. "About Henry Miller." She was still smiling. "But calling the chief Cliffie isn't very nice, Sam."

The day made its appointed rounds. I watched the clouds for a time, remembering the Baudelaire poem loosely translated as "The Wonderful Clouds." So heartbreakingly beautiful. The day we studied it in class I was surrounded by people who absolutely didn't give a damn about it, including the teaching assistant, who, after each poet we studied, always said, "I'll still take Whitman."

I sat and daydreamed. I wished I could paint. Or be a serious pianist. Or be taller. Or handsome. Or be better endowed in the groin department. Or be a great novelist. Or really and truly believe in God. Or figure out a way to get Pamela to marry me. Or stumble over a bag containing $300 million that nobody claimed. You know, the usual modest daydreams.

"I think I'll buy one of these cars, McCain."

The voice was unmistakable: Judge Esme Anne Whitney. She was approaching the park bench where I was lighting a Lucky. Smokes always taste better after food, even half-finished ice-cream cones.

"You're kidding."

"I dated one of the Ford boys."

"So I heard."

"Would you tell Henry that there's a lady here who would like to sit down?"

"Henry, there's a lady here who would like to sit down."

Henry didn't budge. He's one of God's few creatures not intimidated by Judge Whitney.

I helped him down. He didn't look happy. He glared at the Judge, his little sailor's cap angled cutely on his little head and waddled away.

"I doubt he's sanitary," she said.

"He's a lot cleaner than some of my clients," I said.

"I've seen some of your clients," she said, "and I agree."

She didn't ask to sit down. She just sat down. Which was all right with me. I wanted some company, even if it was my boss.

What you have to remember about Judge Whitney is that I don't necessarily like her but then again I don't necessarily *not* like her. And if that's confusing for you, think how confusing it is for *me*.

The Judge is a damned good-looking sixty-year-old woman but, because she's usually so cold and baronial, people don't see that. Fashion-model slender. Poised. Model-like too in the brazen jut of nose and the impudence of eyes and upper lip. Her gray hair is kept short but very feminine. And somehow her tortoiseshell eyeglasses are sexy. She's also got a kid grin that shocks you the first couple of times you see it. She makes three pilgrimages a year to the Holy Land — the high-fashion stores of New York City — where she buys her clothes.

You know, the French designers whose names you can't pronounce at prices your entire block couldn't afford if they pooled their money? Her choice in cigarettes runs to Gauloises and her choice in booze is brandy, which I could smell on her breath. Whatever you do, don't mention Ayn Rand. Rand is her favorite author, and she can give you five extemporaneous hours on the topic. Her major was law but her minor was philosophy.

"Just because you dated one of the Ford boys doesn't mean you have to buy one."

"Well, if I don't, who will?" she asked. She was peering down into the gray suede of her tiny purse, the same gray suede that accented certain spots of her gray sharkskin suit. "It's clear that the ordinary people out here can't see what an important and forward-thinking design concept this is."

She held a handful of four-color brochures, like a poker hand. Which is where that "important and forward-thinking design concept" came from.

"The one mistake the Ford boys made was marketing this beautiful car to the masses," she said. "It was clearly designed by and for the — well, more educated classes, shall we say."

In case you hadn't figured it out yet, Esme

Anne Whitney is a snob. After several brandies, the word *rabble* frequently falls from her lips.

"Look what I found," she said.

Her kid grin. Those baby teeth of hers. She looked pretty cute.

Until I realized that what she found were three rubber bands. She gets some kind of deep dark Freudian sexual pleasure out of shooting rubber bands at me and seeing if I can duck away in time.

But she was only teasing. She dangled the rubber bands so that I could see them and put them back. She was a proper lady after all. Shooting rubber bands should only be done in the privacy of one's office.

"Damn."

"What?"

"I'm out of cigarettes."

"Have one of mine."

"You smoke those American things."

"You smoke those French things."

"Oh, hell, McCain, give me one, I suppose."

I gave her one. I even struck the match for her.

She inhaled deeply. Exhaled. "These are even worse than I remembered." Then: "I clocked you yesterday."

"Clocked me?"

"Loitering at Pamela's desk."

"Oh."

"She's mine, not yours, McCain. At least during business hours."

"I'll try to watch it."

"You always say that. Now I'm afraid I'll have to take action."

"Action?"

"For every minute you stand out there mooning over her, I'm going to dock you a dollar. Given what I pay you, and given how long you moon, you could easily end up owing *me* money." She dropped her Lucky on the ground and twisted it into shreds with the tip of her gray suede high-heeled shoe. "These are terrible. Just terrible." She sat back and said, "Why don't you marry that Mary Travers? It seems to be a much better fit. Pamela has . . . aspirations."

"Ah."

"What in God's name does *ah* mean?"

"It means that even though her family no longer has money, it once did. So you relate to her."

"Sometimes families lose their fortune and then regain it again."

"So I should stick with my kind and Pamela should stick with hers, is that it?"

"No offense, McCain, but you're a man of simple needs. And from what I can see,

Mary Travers — who is very *very* pretty, by the way — is also a person of simple needs."

I was about to tell her how insulting her theory was — to both Mary and me — when I saw Dick Keys pushing through the crowd and shouting my name. He looked crazed. As a young man, he'd distinguished himself by flying more than sixty bombing missions as a tail gunner in World War Two. He was known for his charm, his self-possession.

People were watching him now.

Something was obviously wrong.

He stumbled over somebody's foot and practically landed on his face in front of me.

"Sam, you have to help me," he said, his breath coming in short gasps.

"What's wrong?"

"I'll explain when we get there."

"Hello, Richard," the Judge said loftily. "Or aren't we speaking anymore?"

He seemed to see her for the first time.

"Oh, hi, Judge. God, I'm sorry, I'm just so — confused, I guess. I really need to borrow young McCain here, if you don't mind."

"Consider him borrowed, Richard. But next time you could at least have the courtesy to say hello to me." She was the only person who called him Richard. He apparently brought out the schoolmarm in her.

"I will, Judge, I promise," he said. And

31

then: "C'mon, Sam. Hurry!"

And we were off.

It took us a good seven–eight minutes of broken-field running to get inside the service garage, where we were finally alone.

"What's going on, Dick?"

He looked at me lost in grief. "It's bad enough that everybody hates the Edsel grille because it looks like a woman's vagina. That isn't enough? Now I got a body on my hands."

I really thought he might start crying.

Two

The garage had six bays and smelled wonderfully of oil and grease and cleaning compound. There was no activity today, no wrenches clanging to the floor, no Hank Williams song on the radio, no Pepsi bottles yanked out of the nickel machine in the corner. It was Edsel Day, after all. Only heathens would work on a day like this.

I looked around the silent garage wistfully. I've always wanted to be one of those manly men who can walk into a service garage and know exactly what to do. I'm terrible with hammers, saws, and screwdrivers. My dad learned my terrible secret when I was nine years old and he asked me to help him hang a pair of shutters my mom had bought at Woolworth's. They were supposed to go on either side of the kitchen window. My dad held the shutter in place — which was the hard part of the job — while I was supposed to bang in the first couple of nails. I banged, all right — right through storm window and window alike. My mom jumped back from the sink, screaming, as glass icicles flew everywhere. From then

33

dad always got my kid sister to help him with his carpentry projects.

And that's why I take my ragtop to Denny's garage whenever anything goes wrong. I sure couldn't fix it myself.

"I need you to look at something, Sam."

"What is it?"

"I'll just let you see for yourself."

I looked at all the Rotary good service plaques he had mounted above the desk.

If you've read any Sinclair Lewis — my undergraduate major was American Literature — you know the word *booster*. And boy, that was Dick. He belonged to everything — Rotary, Kiwanis, Eagles, Elks, VFW, Masons, Chamber of Commerce, you name it — and he boosted everything too: high school sports, the new swimming pool, the new softball diamond, and stricter regulation of teenage drinking at both drive-in theaters. His people had come out here from New England in the early 1850s. They brought a lot of good recipes and clean, admirable habits with them, including the principles of education with which the Iowa Territory established its first schools. And they brought along the dulcimer, an instrument till then unknown in these parts. The odd thing was, whenever you saw Dick with his fellow Rotarians or Kiwanians, he seemed apart from them. The smile touched the lips but never the eyes, and the eyes strayed constantly, looking out some window that was his alone.

"C'mon." Then, as we started walking, he said, "You've got a private investigator's license, don't you?"

"Yes."

"And you do work for Judge Whitney?"

"Yes I do."

He sighed. The handsome face looked a little fleshy and old. It was a strange feeling. He seemed older now than he had a few minutes ago. He was Jay Gatsby at fifty-five, and that's no Jay Gatsby at all.

He said, "There's a dead girl in the trunk."

Three Edsels were lined along the rear wall, their trunk ends out. The colors of these three were as silly as the colors of those on the lot: exotic fruity colors that no self-respecting automobile should ever be.

"I was just getting these ready for delivery," he said. "That's why they're in here." He looked paler, grimmer even than before.

I wasn't sure which trunk held the girl until we got close. A bloody handprint was on the fender of the center car, the peach-and-kiwi-colored one.

"That's my handprint, by the way."

Great. The Sykes clan that ran the town and thus the police department didn't need any help being incompetent. But Dick was going to see they got it. I wondered what other parts of the crime scene he'd violated. He saw my expression. "I panicked, McCain. I reached in and touched her to make sure she was dead —"

"That's all right." What the hell. He was having a bad enough day as it was. "The trunk open?"

He nodded.

I got down on my haunches and took my ballpoint out of my white button-down shirt. That style of shirt, chinos, and desert boots are my customary uniform. They give my baby face and diminutive stature at least a semblance of age.

The tip of my ballpoint slid in nicely beneath the trunk catch. I delicately raised the lid. Then I stood up, my knees cracking, and looked inside.

Next to me, Dick said, "She's —"

He didn't finish his sentence. He hiccuped.

"She certainly is."

I recognized her immediately: Susan Squires. Mary Travers had worked for her a couple of years. Susan was married to the

36

then–District Attorney, so they did a lot of entertaining and needed help around the house. Hence, a high school girl like Mary. Inexpensive and tirelessly hardworking. Even more, they were friends, confidantes. You'd see them downtown together, shopping and giggling like girlfriends. Susan told Mary virtually everything about her life.

"She was a pretty gal." Hiccup.

"She sure was."

"And nice. She used to work for me. That's why she was here yesterday, decorating for Edsel Day. A lot of old employees pitched in. This just makes me sick."

"Me too, Mr. Keys."

"And I don't mean just 'cause it'll hurt my business."

I patted him on the shoulder. "You're a good man, Mr. Keys."

He hiccuped.

"Here. Thought you might want this."

He handed me a flashlight.

I played the beam inside the shadowy trunk. She smelled of death. Unclean. This odor fought against the strong smell of the brand-new spare rubber tire. She'd been wearing a blue knee-length skirt and black flats and a white blouse. She had dark hair worn short and was curled up into a kitten ball. The side of her head had been smashed in so brutally you got a few glimpses of clean white bone.

"You're going to have to call the Sykes boys."

Hiccup. "I know I am. But I hate to. They don't have any idea what they're doing." He leaned forward and hiccuped in my face. "That's between you and me."

With all the power the Sykes clan had in this town, a wise man made a point of keeping such opinions to himself.

"Why don't you go call them and I'll look around?"

"I guess I better, huh?"

"Yeah, Dick, you better."

He hiccuped and walked over to a wall phone by a rack of old tires.

I started playing detective.

Cliff Sykes, Jr., had seen one too many Glenn Ford pictures.

You know how Glenn always wears a khaki uniform whenever he plays a lawman? And keeps his gun slung low? And wears tight tan leather gloves? Well, imagine a 250-pound six-foot bullyboy in the same getup, and you've got yourself a picture of Cliff Sykes, Jr. The rest of the force wears standard blue uniforms. But Sykes, being the chief, and his daddy being the richest man in town, gets to play Glenn Ford.

The music stopped as soon as he arrived.

First the live band quit playing. Then the calliope went dead, and then the Ferris wheel music went silent.

And you started to see people at the windows, peering in.

I'd told Keys to lock the doors, just the way I'd learned in the criminology courses I'd taken at the University of Iowa while studying for my private investigator's license. An unadulterated crime scene is the most important part of any murder investigation — short of a confession.

While we were waiting for Cliffie, I walked around the garage. Found nothing interesting. Went outside in back. Found nothing interesting. Walked around the side of the building. And found something. There'd been some kind of accident here last night. A car had backed into the concrete-block edge of the building. Bits of red plastic taillight littered the ground. I got down and picked up a piece. I'd driven over this earlier today. I checked my tires and found the rear left with a sharp angle of glass stuck in it. The tire was quickly going flat.

I walked back to where the taillight pieces lay. Two little kids watched me. One had a

Flash Gordon ray gun that made this really irritating noise every time the trigger was pulled. I tried to avoid them as I sat on my haunches and examined the pieces again.

The kid pulled it thirty or forty times.

"How come you're doing that?" his pacifist pal asked.

"I lost a dime," I said. I didn't want to explain myself.

"If I find it can I have it?" he asked.

I also didn't want to get in a conversation with him.

"You find it, you keep it, how's that?" I asked.

The ray gun shot me several more times, and then they started looking for the dime I hadn't lost.

The taillight pieces belonged to a recent model car. There were two chunks large enough so I recognized the shape. There was also glass, and pieces of chrome trim, on the ground. Flat-tire material. I knew how fussy Dick was about maintaining his lot. If one of his mechanics or customers had lost a taillight this way, it would've been swept up immediately. Meaning they didn't know about it. Meaning it happened last night and they hadn't found it yet.

"Hey, Bobby, look what I found!" I heard one of the kids say, the one without the gun.

He held up a V8 insignia. It was about the size of a fifty-cent piece.

I was just about to ask him for it when a gray suede lady's pump stepped into my view. I followed it up a length of hose, a length of skirt, and a length of matching jacket to the handsome if imperious face of Judge Whitney.

"I assume you're sober, McCain."

"He lost a dime," Bobby said helpfully.

"Pitiful," she said.

I stood up. "I may have found something."

"Something more interesting than a dime, I hope."

The boys started looking for the money again. "How about I give you a dime for what you found?" I said.

"A dime?" Bobby said. "Are you kidding? This is worth at least fifty cents."

"Fifty cents?" his pal with the gun said. "It's worth at least a buck. My dad knows a junk parts place where they buy stuff like this."

Before the price went any higher, I gave them a dollar and took the V8 insignia.

"Now if you only had the rest of the car to go with it," Judge Whitney said. Then: "What's going on?"

I told her.

"Take me inside, McCain."

"You don't want to go in there, Judge."

"And why not?"

"Cliffie's in there."

"Oh."

About the only time they ever saw each other was in her courtroom, when he had to testify against a defendant. Even then they rarely looked at each other and seldom spoke directly.

"I still want to go in."

"You sure?"

"I said so, didn't I?"

We went in a side door.

Cliffie stood in the center of the garage, talking to one of his deputies. Snakeskin boots. A Bowie knife hanging from a scabbard on his belt. A white Stetson hat that would have done John Wayne proud. But the critical part of the image were the eyes. For all his silliness, he was a dangerous man. He'd killed five men in the six years of being chief of police. Not one of them was armed. Most grand juries would take issue with such behavior. But when at least half that grand jury is beholden to your father for their jobs, charges are rarely brought.

He saw her then and she saw him.

It was a Saturday-afternoon Western movie showdown, good versus evil.

True, the judge is arrogant and a snob, and a pain in the ass, and pretentious about her Eastern roots. And yet she's generally fair in the way she dispatches justice. She's an intelligent jurist and a true believer in the Constitution, if that doesn't sound a mite corny in these cynical times.

The Sykeses came here in the last big migration from the Ozarks, which was just after World War One. They ran liquor during prohibition and a variety of black-market items during World War Two. But by a fluke Cliff Sykes, Sr., got a government contract in 1940 to help build training airstrips and barracks for the Army Air Corps, and it made him a millionaire many times over. He was soon building them all over the Midwest. In the process he bought himself the town of Black River Falls. The Judge stayed in office — she was appointed by a state panel that not even Sykes could buy off — but all the appointments she'd made during the Whitney tenure were long gone. The Sykeses ran everything.

Now they faced off.

"He looks dumber than I remembered," the Judge whispered.

Then Cliffie surprised us not only by walking over but by doffing his Stetson and sort of bowing from the hip.

"Judge Whitney," he said. "This is a true pleasure."

"I'd like to offer the services of my own investigator," she said.

He was stunned by her abruptness. So was I. Then he got mad. And then he gave us a grin a lizard would envy. "You have reference to young McCain here?"

"I do indeed. He's a lawyer recognized by the bar and he's also a licensed private investigator who has a passion for modern crime-solving techniques."

"Well, does he now?" The lizard smiled again. "And here I thought he had a passion for that young secretary of yours, Miss Forrest."

"Very funny, Cliffie," I said.

"What'd I'd tell you about calling me that, mister?" he snapped.

"I guess I don't remember," I said.

The Judge said, "The point is, Chief, it doesn't look good for our town to have murders go unsolved. Everybody who can should pitch in. That's why I'm offering you McCain here."

He wouldn't say yes. But he couldn't say no. Because he'd look uncooperative. And he was learning that part of his job was public relations. He no longer beat men in their cells, because that was bad press. Now

44

he took them into the woods, and when they came back he talked about how they'd tried to escape. Cliffie and his father had somehow managed to buy their way into the country club — the last bastion of the Whitneys — and certain amenities were expected of them. No more blowing their noses on the tablecloths.

"I certainly appreciate the offer, Judge. And I certainly will take it under consideration."

The three of us looked up at the man walking quickly toward us, the Judge's number-one nemesis in court. Pure preppy: early thirties, brush-cut blond hair, Brooks Brothers gray three-piece, button-down pink shirt, black tie, graduate of Harvard Law. At one time his parents and the Whitneys had been best friends here in the valley, the only people the Whitneys considered even marginally civilized. Then they'd had a falling out over a business transaction. This had been about the time the Sykes clan had assumed command. The Squires family, no doubt holding their noses, had thrown in with the Sykeses. This was the youngest Squires, David, husband of the dead woman in the trunk of the Edsel. He wore dark glasses and looked like an assassin.

"Aw, David, I'm sure sorry about this," Cliffie said.

"What the hell are *they* doing here?"

He meant us.

"Just talking, I guess."

"Well, I don't want them here."

Much as he was no doubt enjoying himself, even Cliffie had to wonder about a lawyer who would draw down on a judge he frequently appeared before.

"Get them out of here, Cliff. Now."

"Yessir, David." To us: "I guess I have to ask you folks to leave."

Squires was already walking over to the car where two of our town's finest were pawing all over everything without first dusting for fingerprints.

Cliffie doffed his hat again and started to turn away. Then he turned back to us. "Oh, McCain, I seen you outside with that busted taillight stuff. We'll take care of that. Now I'd better see to Mr. Keys."

After I got one of the mechanics to put on my spare, I walked the Judge back to the courthouse.

It was so warm it was hard to imagine that jack-o'-lanterns were only a month away, the smell of fresh-carved pumpkin in the kitchen and scarecrows ready to stalk the twilight land, crows on their ragged shoulders and eerie bogeyman gleams in the vacancy of their eyes. That's why I always kept a Ray Bradbury paperback near my bed. It's fun to be scared that way.

When we got to the courthouse I remembered an article I'd recently read in *The Iowan* about an 1851 trial held in the original version of this Greek-revival building. Seems Black River Falls had been visited by a gang of outlaws on the run from Missouri. They took a liking to the place and stayed for a week or so. They drank, they gambled, they fought. They were in and out of jail. During a card game, a hayseed of eighteen accused the gang, rightly, of cheating. The leader of the gang shot and killed him. All who had seen it insisted that the boy had lunged at the outlaw. The Judge said it would be hard to indict the gang leader, even though the boy had been unarmed. Two nights later, the boy's seventeen-year-old sister confronted the gang leader and shot him dead. A trial was held; there was a hung jury. The judge said the girl committed murder, and to be true to the law you have to convict her; the jurors reluctantly did so. But that night the judge himself appeared at the rear of the jail where the young woman was being kept. He'd outfitted a horse for her, and he gave her enough money and provisions to make it to Minnesota. The girl was never seen again, and no one ever went after her. Her name had been Helen, and she grew so mythic in the minds of the settlers that they called their county Helena.

"You saw him squirm?"

"I saw him squirm. That was a great idea, Judge, asking him if he wanted me to pitch in."

"He'll take it under consideration."

"He wasn't too happy when I called him Cliffie."

"And Squires wasn't very happy to see us."

"He sure wasn't."

"It was one of the few times he could challenge me and get away with it."

When we reached the steps, she said, "I want to humiliate Sykes, McCain."

"I figured you did."

"I want to really rub his face in it."

It was the only way a Whitney could get back at a Sykes these days. A series of embarrassments.

"Do I have time for a beer first?"

"One," she said. "And no more."

"How about two?"

"Two and you'll be asleep. You're a terrible drinker, McCain."

She strode up the courthouse steps, used her Saturday key on the door, and went inside.

Three

Elmer's Tap is a working-class tavern where my dad and I play shuffleboard two or three times a week. Elmer, the owner, refuses to let rock and roll be put on his jukebox so the music runs to Teresa Brewer, Frankie Laine, and The Four Lads. I'm old enough to appreciate that kind of music but it'd still be nice to have Little Richard rattle the windows once in a while.

On a football Saturday when the Hawkeyes had a home game, most of Elmer's regulars were in Iowa City in the stands. Elmer is in his late sixties but still strong enough to throw around large kegs of beer. Thirty years ago he was the state executioner. This was when he lived in Fort Madison, where the hangings were done. He won't talk about it unless he's drunk, which isn't often, and then he's clinical about it. He keeps a hangman's noose tacked to the wall above his cash register. Sentimental, I guess. Every once in a while you'll catch him staring off into the past, that window we all carry around with us, and you wonder if he's thinking about what it was like, killing those men, and if he ever sees them in his dreams. He was a swabbie in the war, with the anchor tattoos to prove it. Maybe they ward off evil dreams of trapdoors flying open.

The stools along the bar were empty. Elmer was washing glasses, a cigarette in the corner of his mouth, the smoke stinging his eyes so that he kept blinking. He was a scrawny man with thick glasses. He was also a Taft Republican. One night my dad and I made the mistake of telling some of the regulars that we didn't think much of Joe McCarthy. A couple of the drunker ones tried to pick fights with us, but Elmer broke it up and said there were three things you should never discuss: "Politics, religion, and the size of your dick, 'cause you don't want to make everybody jealous." Words to live by.

"How they hangin', McCain?" he managed to say around his cigarette. He didn't seem to know anything about the Squires woman. I decided to let him find out on his own. I didn't want to go through it all again.

"Oh, pretty good. How about a Falstaff in the bottle?"

With a soapy hand, he jerked the cigarette from his mouth and dropped it to the floor, where he proceeded to smash it with his foot as if it were a particularly pesky bug.

He got me my beer.

"Shit," he said. "You hear that?"

The radio said it was halftime and the Hawkeyes were down by seven.

"This was supposed to be a Rose Bowl year." Then: "How come you don't like sports, anyway?"

"My heart can't take the excitement." I'd always preferred books. This may have explained my distrust of Joe McCarthy. Why couldn't he have been a Baptist? Why did he have to embarrass the rest of us Irish Catholics?

He smirked and shook his head and then said, "That buddy of yours is puttin' them away."

I looked along the opposite wall where the booths ran all the way to the back. I didn't see anybody.

"He's on the inside of the last booth so you can't see him. Cronin. Somethin's really got him down."

I was going to be Jeff Cronin's best man in less than a month. What was going on?

I decided to find out. I picked up my beer and went back there.

The booth was wood. It had been painted a few years back. A few of the dirty words scrawled into it I didn't understand. But they sure sounded foul.

I sat down. He didn't seem to see me. Just stared at his beer. His head was bobbing. He'd had enough to start losing muscular control.

"Jeff?"

He looked up. "Hi."

"You all right?"

"Pretty drunk, actually."

"Yeah. I kind of noticed that."

Jeff Cronin was a big guy. Everybody always said he should have played football but he was slow and clumsy. His father bred horses, and horses were Jeff's love. He was one of four local veterinarians. He wore a blue sweatshirt. His blond hair was ragged. He hadn't shaved. "Marriage is off, buddy."

"What?"

"Off. O-f-f."

"Off? What the hell're you talking about?"

"Off. That so hard to understand? Off."

"But why?"

"Because I said so, that's why."

It was one of those moments of unreality we all have once in a while. The people and the place look familiar, but something makes you think you're in a parallel universe where everything is subtly different.

Eight–nine years Cronin had been going out with Linda Granger, and three–four years they'd been engaged, and now the wedding was suddenly off?

The dating possibilities in Black River Falls are limited. In our high school class, for instance, there were twenty-two boys and eighteen girls. That isn't a huge base to pick a mate from, especially when you eliminate the ones who find you obnoxious, the ones who find you ugly, the ones who find you boring, and the ones who find you embarrassing. In my case, that left with me a six-girl potential, Pamela and Mary included. The alternative, to increase the mate pool, was to date someone younger or older. Boys tended to date someone younger, girls someone older. Or you could date someone from Crowley, which was twenty miles away, who we beat the shit out of every year in basketball, making it all right for us to date them. Or Nashburn, which was thirty miles away, who beat *us* every year in basketball, making it *not* all right to date *them*.

Cronin, the drunk guy in front of me, the guy who kept reeling around even though he was sitting down, had accomplished the most amazing feat of all: right in our very own class he'd discovered a girl who was (a) nice, (b) smart, and (c) very pretty. And who also just happened to have a pair of knockers that should be enshrined somewhere, the Boobs Hall of Fame, perhaps, which I believe, if I'm not mistaken, is somewhere in Pennsylvania.

And here was Cronin, that very same ungrateful drunk guy, sitting in front of me telling me the marriage was off and giving me the impression that he was the one who'd called it off.

"What the hell's going on, Jeff?"

"It doesn't matter."

"The hell it doesn't."

He stared some more at his glass. "Only friends a man should have are animals. They never let you down."

"Linda's never let you down. She's a good woman."

Glaring at me. "She is, huh? You know that for a fact?"

"Yeah. I do. I've known her all my life. She's a good woman, just like I said."

"Well, old buddy, I guess there's good and there's good, isn't there?"

When you're drunk, you think you're just full of profundities.

"What the hell's that mean, Jeff?"

"It means what it means."

"Thanks for clearing it up."

"Wedding's off."

"Yeah, you said that."

As big a guy as he was, and a pretty good

drinker too, he must have been putting them away a long time. He was about ready to pass out. I doubted he'd had breakfast.

"You can't drive like this."

"Hell if I can't."

"You'll wake up in the drunk tank if you do. And you might kill somebody in the process."

"I wouldn't mind killing somebody about now."

Tears came without any warning. No big sob scene, just the tears of a guy unskilled in the ways of letting go with the gentler emotions. "And right now the person I'd like to kill is myself."

Those were his last words for a while.

His face hit the table pretty hard, knocking over his beer glass. It was empty.

I leaned out of the booth. "Elmer?"

"Yeah?"

"You give me a hand?"

"Passed out, huh?"

"Yeah."

"I shoulda cut him off."

"Yeah, you shoulda."

He came over.

It was hell getting Jeff into my car.

Four

My office is a single room on the side of the local dime store. You reach it by climbing three untrustworthy wooden steps.

On the tiny porch was a small white box with a white envelope Scotch-taped to it: MR. MCCAIN. I carried it inside.

The reason I work for Judge Whitney is so I can afford such luxuries as indoor plumbing, electric lights, and a mattress. In a town with too many lawyers already, a tyro doesn't exactly get the highest-paying clients.

Take this little box. Helen Reynolds, a sweet weary woman who cleans rooms out at the Sunset Motel, has a fifteen-year-old son who has been in and out of trouble with the law since he was twelve. Mostly minor offenses: toilet-papering the trees of girls he has crushes on, overturning garbage cans in alleys, and writing dirty words on the sides of buildings. Buggsy Siegel he's not. But he seems to be in court every month or so. Maybe if his dad hadn't died in Korea the kid would've turned out better. You never know about those things and you can make an argument either way. Anyway, none of the other lawyers will take his cases. No money in them. Helen lives in a two-room apartment and drives a 1948 Hudson, one of the big ones that looks like an overturned bathtub. So I take his cases. And in lieu of pay she makes me angel food cakes with a lot of nice frosting on them. Every three–four weeks I get one. This was my payment on account.

The mail was three overdue bills, an invitation to a séance Halloween party (*Maybe Bridey Murphy will be there!*) thrown by a very successful tort lawyer, and a note folded in half.

Hi McCain — I need to talk to you. Called and stopped by.
                                    Mary

Mary Travers is the girl I should marry. She's smart, sweet, sensible, and as good-looking in her dark-haired way as Pamela Forrest is in her blond-haired way. She had a straight-A average in high school and had hopes for college, but then her dad got sick so she had to stay home and help support the family. She works the lunch counter down at the Rexall. A couple of nights, especially on high school graduation night, we came close to going all the way. She'd caught the McCain virus in junior high just as I'd caught the Pamela virus in fourth grade. And neither of us could find a cure. There was a time, right after high school, when she pursued me actively. But no more. I ate lunch at the Rexall a few times a week, and those were the only times I'd see her. The way she looked at me, I knew she still loved me. And the way I looked at her, she knew I was still in love with Pamela. We were miserable.

I had just sliced myself a piece of cake with my letter opener when the phone rang.

"Hi, McCain."

"Hi, Mary. I got your note."

"I knew Susan Squires really well."

"That's right. You did."

"I wondered if we could get together and talk."

A ruse for a sort of date?

"Sure."

"You could stop by the house."

The house she referred to was the one she'd grown up in in the Knolls. My dad had gotten a good job after the war and we'd moved to a new house in one of the thousands of Levittown-style developments that had spread across the country. Washers and dryers. A new car every couple of years. A

TV antenna on the roof. Steak once a week. The GI Bill. A chance for your kids to go to college. Uncle Miltie. Howdy Doody. Ed Sullivan. The promise of America, especially to those who had grown up in the despair of the Depression and had gone off to war.

A lot of returning GIs did well but Mary's dad had not. He'd seen Japanese soldiers slice up his friends with machetes and then hang them like slabs of beef off palm trees. He had a "nervous condition." Couldn't hold any job long. Went into depressions so bad they had to put him in the bughouse a couple of times. And now he had cancer. Mary still lived at home to help him and her mother, who wasn't all that healthy either. I felt terrible about not being in love with Mary. Sometimes I got down on my knees and actually prayed that I'd stop loving Pamela and start loving Mary. That'd make so many people happy. Including me.

"There's a hayrack ride tonight," I said.

"I saw that."

"You want to go?"

"Are you serious? With me?"

"Sure. I'll pick you up at seven."

"That's only three hours, McCain."

"You'll look beautiful; you always do."

"I was going to tell you about Susan."

"Tell me tonight."

"I'd feel guilty going. With Susan dead and all."

"It's just what you need."

"I guess it probably is."

I could hear how happy I'd made her, and that made me happy. Maybe I couldn't fall *in* love with her but I loved her.

"Seven o'clock then."

I was just turning off the desk lamp when the knock came. A client. A small practice like mine, they just drop by when they need to. Most of the time it's all right. But now I had things to do.

"C'mon in."

I knew the moment I saw her what was going to happen. You don't run into that many Gaelic goddesses. It's probably the hair: a bloody mane of it, the color of red at the epicenter of a fire and reaching all the way down to the sleekly jutting hips. A white silk blouse and no bra, a pair of tight tan slacks resembling jodhpurs and tucked into a smashing pair of knee-length riding boots, and a face as erotic and innocent as those photography magazines with the young women of Paris. Maggie Yates. The twenty-eight-year-old would-be writer everyone in town loved to gossip about. No bra was bad enough, but she also wrote letters to the local paper defending communism, marijuana, and pornography. Every male in town over the age of ten lusted after her but she would tryst only with me, as she frequently said, "Because even though you're no genius, McCain, you at least know who Isadora Duncan is." She lived above a garage on an allowance and was finishing up a novel she said was a combination of *Peyton Place* and *The Dubliners*. She went to the Writers' Workshop in Iowa City for a semester and dropped out to write. She is being supported by a fashion-model sister in New York who sends her a check and cast-off clothes once a month (hence the expensive duds). Her parents died when she was young, and she has made mention of a trust fund that will someday be hers, the source of which is — mysterious. But then eastern money is always mysterious, you make money on money, on embosed sheets of paper. Out here you amass money through substantial and three-dimensional ways, with corn, cows, or ointments for pig hemorrhoids.

"I was just downtown," she said, "and wanted to see if you were busy tonight." Then: "God, I've got to get out of this town."

"Why?"

"Why? Did you hear what I just said? *I was*

just downtown? There *isn't* any downtown here, McCain, just three or four blocks of really pathetic old stores. I'm starting to sound like I *belong* in this place." She shook her head. "God, as soon as I finish my novel, I'm heading straight back to New York."

"I'm in kind of a hurry."

She grinned. "How much of a hurry?"

She'd caught me staring at her breasts.

"Well, you know. A hurry."

"You just wet your lips and gulped."

"Oh?"

"Yeah. And you know what that means, don't you?"

"What?"

"That you're horny."

"Why does it mean that?"

"Because your crotch just moved too. That thing of yours is bouncing around in there."

I sighed. "Well, can I tell you I like you?"

"Aw, McCain, we've talked and talked about that."

"It just makes me feel better is all."

"You're so old-fashioned."

"Yeah, I probably am."

"Did you read that Françoise Sagan novel I gave you?"

"Uh-huh."

"Well, didn't you notice how people're always doing it and they *never* tell each other that they like each other? That's a sign of true sophistication. Going all over the place and screwing people you hate."

"They're French."

"What's that got to do with it?" she said.

"The French're capable of anything. Look at World War Two. How long did they hold out, an hour and a half?"

This time, *she* sighed. "OK, but you can only say it once."

"That's good enough for me. Let's hop to it."

So we hopped to it. Pleasuring her was a pleasure. But fornicate we did. She was some fornicator she was. She'd taught me any number of things about lovemaking, things I longed to try out on Pamela. Things I was sure that stupid rich handsome and successful Stu would never know.

The fornication was, as always, great. She smelled good, tasted good, moved good, whispered good. As soon as we finished, she started to push me away. "Thanks, McCain. That was nice."

"Wait a minute. You didn't let me say it yet."

"Aw, shit, I forgot. Hurry up, will you? My butt's starting to freeze."

I looked at her gorgeous eyes. She was incomprehensible to me. A creature from a future world. Most girls not only begged but demanded some choice words of *amour* afterward. She despised them.

"Can't you at least *pretend* you like it?" I said.

"Just hurry *up.*"

I was still in the saddle and it felt wonderful; it's as good a place to be as there is, and I wanted to stay there for a minute or two, maybe joke around a little or something, but I knew I had to hurry so I said, "I really do like you, Maggie. You're crazy and you scare the shit out of me but I'm fascinated by you and I like the *hell* out of you and I can't help it."

"Great," she said, giving me a shove.

We dressed on either side of the desk. Underwear elastic snapping. Feet stomped into shoes. Zippers running their patterns.

She was all dressed and lighting a Camel when she said, "By the way, you know that prick David Squires, his wife just got killed."

"Yeah?"

"I ever tell you he put the make on me one night at his summer home?"

"You're kidding."

"Uh-uh. Wanted me to go down in the

basement with him. Told me it was a lot of fun to do it standing up. Just like Hemingway did, he said. I guess he was trying to impress me with his vast knowledge of literature."

"How'd he know Hemingway did it standing up?"

"I guess because of that scene in *A Farewell to Arms*."

"Oh, yeah, I forgot."

"What a jerk."

"Hemingway?"

"No, Squires. He's this big capital-punishment jerk. Schmuck. I'd like to capital-punish *him* sometime."

That was another cool thing about Maggie Yates. She knew all these great Yiddish words from New York. Hearing them and saying them made *me* feel very cool.

I started to kiss her good-bye but remembered that a good-bye kiss was another no-no.

"See you, McCain," she said. And was out the door.

So David Squires had put the make on her. Interesting. What if he were a chaser? What bearing might that have on this case?

On the way over to Keys Ford-Lincoln, I listened to the national radio news. The big

Edsel Day had been something of a bust all over the country. A lot of people had found the car ugly. And a lot more found it over-priced.

The cleaning crew was already at work on the grounds. There were dead balloons and pennants and Pepsi cups and gum wrappers and cigarette butts covering the tarmac everywhere. The celebration had been scheduled to last until evening with a country-western band and a barbecue. Dick had obviously called it off.

No police cars. Cliffie had done his usual thorough job. The body had been discovered less than four hours ago and Cliffie was already long gone.

I wheeled the ragtop around back and went in the service door. Keys's big yellow Lincoln convertible was parked nearby so I assumed he was still there.

He was there, all right. In his office. With a cigar and a bottle of Wild Turkey that he was pouring straight into a Pepsi paper cup. He had his shirt open, his tie off, and his cordovan Florsheim wing tips up on his desk.

His wife sat on the edge of a wooden chair. She wore a green dress that looked light enough for summer. For such a big-boned woman, she moved with appealing grace. Her perch on the chair was delicate.

"I feel like calling Edsel Ford at home," he said, "and telling him what a piece of shit his car is."

"I *still* like it," his wife said. "But obviously the public doesn't share my taste." She rose. "Well, dear, I'm going to go spend some of your money."

"Buy me a couple of gallons of bourbon," he said.

She winked at me. "Be sure he doesn't do anything foolish, Sam."

He made a sound that faintly resembled a laugh. "I do foolish things all the time. Nobody's been able to stop me yet." The bitterness surprised me. She looked embarrassed by it.

She nodded to both of us and left.

"Damn, she's a nice lady," Keys said. "Don't know why the hell she puts up with me." Then: "Drink?"

"No, thanks."

He gunned some more of his own.

He sighed. "First the Edsel. And now Susan Squires."

"Yeah, I was meaning to ask about her. She used to work here, you said?"

"Two years. Back when she dropped out of college."

My question didn't seem to surprise him

at all. "Was she seeing David Squires while she worked here?"

"The last year or so. He was here so often, I damn near offered to put him on payroll."

"I take it you didn't like it."

"She was the receptionist. She had to meet people and be nice to them. Most people don't appreciate how important a good receptionist is. They're your first contact with the public. A receptionist who is rude or unhelpful gives you a bad impression of the place."

"Was she rude and unhelpful?"

"She wasn't rude very often. But unhelpful, yes. At least for the last six–seven months she worked here. She was caught up in her affair with Squires. They'd have an argument and she'd come in to work looking teary and worn out. Started calling in sick a lot. You know how it is when you're in love. Sometimes you have a hard time concentrating. And he's still married all this time. You'd think they would've been a little more discreet."

"Yeah," I said, thinking of Pamela and her affair with Stu. "Yeah, you would."

"I didn't want to fire her. But I was glad when she finally quit."

"Because of the scandal?"

"Hell, yes. It wasn't real good for business, believe me. She just couldn't take it anymore. She went to stay with some relative. By that time, I sure as hell didn't blame her."

"Why was she here now?"

"Oh, hell, we're still friends. After she and Squires finally got married and everything settled down, she dropped in all the time. Everybody here still liked her."

I was writing all this down in my notebook.

"What's wrong with Howdy Doody?" he asked.

"Huh?"

"Your notebook. Noticed you've got a Captain Video. They out of Howdy Doody, were they?"

I felt my cheeks burn. "I got a deal on these."

"Musta been some deal" — he smiled — "make you carry a notebook like that around. Captain Video, I mean."

I changed the subject. "Cliffie spend much time here?"

"They're having corn on the cob over at the Eagles tonight and then showing two Abbott and Costello pictures. Cliffie's like a kid about that kind of stuff. You think he'd hang around and do his job when they've got corn on the cob boiling in those big pots?"

The office was small. He had a lot of family photos on the wall and a badly thrumming Pepsi machine in the corner. There were also more plaques, these from the Ford Motor Company, one of them having to do with clean rest rooms. Not the kind of thing you'd want on your tombstone: HE KEPT A CLEAN JOHN.

"You notice if he did anything with that broken taillight cover?"

"He didn't. I asked my boys if they knew anything about it and they didn't. Gil said it wasn't there when he left last night at seven but it was here this morning when he came in at six."

"So Cliffie didn't take it?"

"Far as I know, he didn't even look at it. Think the cleaning crew finally picked it up and tossed it in one of the cans out back."

"Mind if I look?"

"That's some job you've got, McCain. Scrounging around in waste cans."

"I didn't get a law degree for nothing."

He laughed. "Yeah, and everybody in this town is proud of you." Then: "Poor Susie. Just can't figure out how she got in that Edsel. Why couldn't it have been the Pontiac dealer down the street? I know that sounds sort of mean, but between the bad publicity with the Edsel and the murder. . . ."

Sure you don't want a drink?"

"No, thanks. I've got to put that law degree of mine to use."

He smiled. "Thanks for making me feel better, McCain. I appreciate it."

The sky was darker now, stains of mauve and gold and amber, a few thunderheads brilliantly outlined with the last of the day's sunlight. There's a loneliness to Saturday night, at least for me, that no amount of noise and movement can ever assuage. There're a lot of popular songs about Saturday night, about how you live all week for it to roll around so you can go out and have yourself a ball. But deep down you know it'll never be quite as exciting as you want it to be, *need* it to be, and the lonesomeness will never quite go away. I think my mom used to feel this when my dad was in Europe during the war. She'd kind of fix herself up on Saturday night and then sit in the living room by herself with her one highball in her hand and a Chesterfield in her fingers. Even when she'd laugh at the radio jokes there'd be a lonesomeness in her eyes that made me sad for her and scared for my dad. But we were lucky. Dad came home.

There were five large trash barrels out back. A big lonely mutt hung around watching me.

It took me twenty minutes to find what I was looking for. I couldn't decide whether to start on the barrels from the left or right. If I'd started from the left I would have been out of there in five minutes. So of course I started from the right. This is the kind of frustration that the nuns always said was good for us. Taught us humility and patience. I never was sure about that. It was like attributing not eating meat on Friday to Jesus. All the things that poor guy had on his mind, did he really have time to worry about cheeseburgers?

By the time I finished, my shirtsleeves were grimy and my fingernails were black. In the center of the fourth barrel, I found what I was looking for. Whoever had picked it up had been thoughtful enough to put it in a paper bag for me. Even the little pieces.

"OK, now, McCain. Close your eyes."

Mrs. Goldman is a widow who rents out rooms. I'd call her my landlady, but that term always paints a mental picture of a dowdy middle-aged woman with flapping house slippers and pink curlers in her hair. Unless of course you read the occasional Midwood "adult" novels they sell under the counter down at Harkin's News. In those books landladies are invariably twenty years old and cursed with nymphomania and they're always asking the narrator if he'd "like to earn a little discount on his rent."

I figure Lauren Bacall will probably look like Mrs. Goldman when she reaches her mid-fifties: tall, elegant, quietly imposing. Mrs. Goldman's husband died six years ago. She hasn't had a single date since. Until tonight. She goes to temple in Iowa City every Saturday. She recently met an optometrist there, a man around sixty and a widower. He was taking her out for steaks and dancing tonight.

"Ready?"

"Ready, Mrs. Goldman."

"And you'll be honest?"

"Absolutely."

Mrs. Goldman keeps the downstairs for herself. There are three apartments upstairs. She'd bought herself some new duds and wanted my opinion of them. I'd never seen her this nervous before. It was cute.

"Here I come, ready or not!"

She came down the hall from the bedroom into the living room and she was gorgeous. Really. She'd bought a black shift and black hose and black pumps and one of those little French-style hats that Audrey Hepburn wears whenever she wants to get

William Holden all hot and bothered.

"Holy moly."

"You think he'll like it?"

"Are you kidding? He'll break down in tears."

She smiled. "You never overstate things, McCain. That's one of your finest qualities." She leaned over and gave me a motherly kiss on the cheek. "I appreciate the compliment. I need it. I keep running to the bathroom every five minutes, just the way I used to when I started dating my husband. I have a bladder that's very sensitive to romantic feelings."

She smelled great too.

Then: "Oh. David Squires stopped by to see you."

"David Squires? Are you sure it was him?"

She laughed. "Are you saying that I should have Dr. Kostik check my eyes tonight? I know David from the Fine Arts committee at the library."

"God," I said, stunned. "Why would he want to see me? He and the Judge despise each other."

"That's what I was thinking. But his wife was murdered, so maybe he needs to talk to you. The poor man."

Five

Dillon's Stables had a huge red barn for dances and three big hayracks for rides. I wore a T-shirt, a denim jacket, jeans, and desert boots. To get in the Western mood I wore a red kerchief around my neck.

Mary was dressed in a similar outfit. Her mahogany-colored hair was pulled back into a ponytail. A hundred male eyes did terrible things to her. She was a beauty. No doubt about that.

From inside the barn came music: Jerry Lee Lewis, Gene Vincent, Buddy Holly. This was a young crowd tonight. If Dillon had his way he'd still be playing songs from the '40s. Fortunately, his twenty-year-old daughter chose the music. Just because you dressed Western didn't mean you had to listen Western. Especially when you had your hair swept back into a duck's ass.

The hayracks filled up pretty fast. Mary and I got on the third one. We sat high on the stack, about four feet up. A friendly old mare pulled the wagon, following an ancient Indian trail along a creek painted silver by moonlight. The night was chilly, the hay smelled fresh and clean, and the mare was sweetly scented of field dust and road apples.

"Did you ever try and count the stars?" Mary asked.

"Not after they let me out of the mental hospital."

She nudged me. She had a cute way of doing that. She'd done it since grade school. For some reason I've always taken great pleasure in being nudged by her.

"They made me do that at Girl Scout camp. Sit up all night and count the stars."

"Nice girls."

"Yeah, but I was dumb enough to do it."

There were six other couples. One of the guys had a guitar. He played some Gene Autry and Roy Rogers songs, and then he played Vaughn Monroe's "Ghost Riders in the Sky." I still like to lie on my stomach and look out the window to see if I can spot any of the ghost riders he sings in that song. It isn't hard to spot them. Not if you had an imagination like mine. Big silver ghost horses and cow-pokes trailing across the midnight sky.

"She was a nice woman."

"Susan Squires?"

"Ummm."

"Why'd she marry him?"

"She was in love with him."

"Poor girl."

Some of the other couples were already making out. A Tribute to Gonads seemed to be the theme of the evening. I had my arm around Mary but that was it.

"She stopped in for lunch at Rexall," Mary said.

"When?"

"About a week ago."

"She say anything?"

"She just kept toying with an envelope. She was so nervous, she left it behind."

"Anything on the outside?"

"Just the return address for a county courthouse. I've got it at home. She called later that afternoon. Sounded scared. Wanted to meet me for a Coke downtown. But Dad got very sick. They're trying this new medication on him. I had to help Mom."

"That was the last you heard from her?"

"Yes. Now I feel guilty. I mean, I had to help Dad and Mom. But I feel as if I let Susan down."

"You sure she sounded scared?"

"Positive. I knew her well enough to know that."

"Know much about her marriage?"

Before she could answer, the wagon gave a sudden jerk and stopped. We had crested a hill. Below us spread the town of Black River

Falls. This should have been the makeout point of choice for all the town's teenagers, but the mud-ribbed roads and brambled roadsides made it too hard to get to.

The sight was gorgeous. If you grew up in a city, a town of 25,000 probably doesn't look like much. But spread out this way, the lights vivid against the prairie night, it was a lovely spectacle. For all its flaws and shortcomings, I loved the old town. Back in the stables, they had a wall posted with photos of various generations who had gone on hayrack rides, all the way back to the 1880s, when the men wore bowlers and the women wore huge picture hats. There were doughboys from World War One and dogfaces from World War Two. There were flappers and Frank Sinatra's bobby-soxers and Johnnie Ray's teary teens. And somehow I was a part of it, just like Mom and Dad and Sis and Grandad and Grandma were part of it, and that made at least a little sense of life for me, being part of a town and a tradition, and if that was all I ever got, it was enough.

Then we were moving again, the wagon jostling left and right, bouncing up and down, the kid with the guitar singing a Frankie Laine song called "Moonlight Gambler." He did a pretty good job of it too.

"She ever talk about her marriage?"

"Just kind of hinted about it from time to time."

"Anything specific?"

"Well, that he spent a lot of time away from home. His legal practice and everything."

"Ever mention divorce?"

"No."

"His ex-wife ever get over it?"

"You think she might have killed ~~him~~ her?"

"It's a thought."

"Gee, I hadn't even considered her."

"Susan ever mention the woman's confronting her or anything?"

"Say," she said, "you're right! One day at Nicole's." Nicole's On Main was the high-fashion emporium of the town. They have indoor plumbing and everything. "She came right up to Susan and slapped her."

"See? There you go. You could be a detective."

"Oh, sure."

"Well, you just told me something very important."

Right there we were headed into the white birches where the creek widens out. The Mesquakie Indians used to call the birches ghost trees, and that's what they looked like, too, with their spectral moonlit glow.

Then I surprised both of us by leaning over and kissing her.

As I've told you, a couple of times we almost went all the way, Mary and I. One was the night of our high school graduation and the second time was just a regular night at the drive-in watching a couple of really bad Japanese science-fiction movies. Both times both of us pulled back. Our relationship was complicated enough. I'd wanted to sleep with her for many long years but I was worried that it would hurt her.

But within five minutes tonight I was on first base and rounding toward second. And in her sweet, somewhat tentative way I sensed she was as up for it as I was.

We sank into the hay and did some serious making out. A hoot owl and a coyote crooned to the moon to lend everything a note of prairie romance.

I always carried my emergency red Trojan, and I had reason to believe that my erection would soon start making overtures in that direction. Bad enough I wasn't in love with Mary. But to make love to her and *still* not be in love with her would be awful.

"We'd better stop," I whispered.

"Oh, God, why?"

"You know."

"Oh, McCain, c'mon. I'm twenty-two years old. You want to see my driver's license?"

"It'll just make things worse."

"For whom?"

"For you. *And* me."

"For you, you mean. The guilt."

But by then the point was moot. A private plane was buzzing the wagon and everybody on the loft was waving. Mary got embarrassed suddenly and eased me away.

By the time we got back to the barn, I was so charged up with lust I had lost the use of my eyes, ears, and nose. I was virtually insensate.

I went into the men's room — a stall; standing at a trough with a hard-on was apt to get you some funny looks — and commanded my penis to cease and desist. I threatened lawsuits; I hinted at solitary confinement. And it finally complied.

Mary had used the time to freshen up. We'd both had to de-hay ourselves the way you have to de-tick yourself after a walk in the woods.

She looked even better than before. And she loved me. And she was tender and smart and faithful and would make a great wife and great mother and — why had God saddled me with Pamela? Why? Oral Robbers could heal people, supposedly. Maybe he could cure me of Pamela. It was something to think about anyway.

The dance pavilion was built right onto the east side of the barn.

We danced fast to a Rick Nelson song and then slow to a Patti Page song and then we went over to the bar and ordered two Falstaffs in the bottle. A bartender with a big ragged straw hat and a piece of hay sticking out of his mouth served us. From what I could hear around us, the conversation this evening was Susan Squires's death.

"I hope this doesn't make me sick."

Mary wasn't much of a drinker.

"Then don't drink it."

"Well, I like to feel like an adult every once in a while." She slid her hand in mine. "That was a lot of fun. On the hayrack."

"It sure was."

"I just wish you didn't worry about stuff so much."

"So do I."

"If you're worried about breaking my heart, McCain, I'm the only one responsible. I could've walked away a long time ago."

A Little Richard song came on. Most of the people were on the dance floor and I mean they were wailing and flailing. I wonder what our ancestors would have thought — you know, the ones who always look so prim in those 1880 photographs — if they could have seen my generation cavort. Probably put the lot of us in the public stocks.

I slid my arm around her. Pushed my face into her lustrous and sweet-smelling hair.

"I'm very seriously in like with you," I said.

"Well." She smiled. "That's a start anyway."

"Hi, Mary."

The words came over my shoulder. I saw Mary's face as they were spoken. She seemed less than happy to see the speaker.

"Hi, Todd."

He walked around me where I could see him.

Our town was getting just big enough that it was impossible to know everybody's name. I'd seen him around, a big towheaded guy who could've doubled for the hearty lumberjack on a cereal box. He even dressed that way. Plaid shirt with the sleeves rolled up, big studded belt, jeans. I was just happy he wasn't carrying an ax. He looked to be about my age. He also looked to be drunk.

"You goin' to the funeral?" he said to Mary.

"Of course."

"I can't decide. Her folks don't like me much."

"I wonder why." Then: "Todd Jensen. This is Sam McCain."

He didn't acknowledge me in any way.

"Maybe if she'd married me instead of him, she wouldn't be dead."

"Meaning what exactly?"

"You figure it out."

"That her husband killed her?"

"You figure it out. She treated me like shit."

"And you were always such a prince."

"Bitch lied to me."

"Why don't you just leave, Todd? She was my friend."

"You always treated me like shit too."

"Good-bye, Todd."

And then he was gone, wobbling off down the bar, people just naturally making room for his hulking body.

"Friend of yours?"

"Oh, sure. Couldn't you tell how happy I was to see him? He was Susan's old boyfriend, believe it or not. She went out with him for six or seven months before she met David Squires. He was one of those insanely jealous guys. She had to account for every single minute she wasn't with him. He used to follow her around until she caught him at it one night. When they broke up, he used to call her ten times a night. And when she started seeing David Squires, he started sending her threatening letters. Squires had Cliffie pay him several visits, but he still wouldn't lay off. Finally, Squires wrote a letter to the local medical association in Cedar Rapids."

"Medical association?"

"Yes. Believe it or not, Todd's a doctor."

"No surgical tools for that guy. He just tears your liver out when he wants to examine it."

"Anyway, he seemed finally to give up. Then about four months ago, the threatening letters started again. Susan was sure it was Todd." Then: "How about a dance?"

"My feet are at your command."

Then I saw him.

At first I wasn't sure I was seeing right: Mike Chalmers? I used to play sandlot baseball with him until he stole my bike one day and tried to blame it on a kid who hung around the diamond. That's how Mike's life ran, one scrape after another. Stealing bikes. Stealing money from cash registers. Stealing cars. Breaking and entering. Finally, armed robbery. He'd gotten out of prison a couple of years back.

Chalmers, a slight man with a hard

peasant handsomeness, smirked at me and then looked away.

"Friend of yours?" Mary asked.

"I helped send him up."

"God, I'd hate to have your job." Then: "He looks kind of sad, doesn't he?"

"Yeah," I said. "Yeah, he does."

We were slow-dancing to a Pat Boone song when I glanced out one of the barn windows and got the idea for the taillight check. There had to be a couple of hundred cars here this evening, maybe one of them with a broken taillight. I was going to get an early A.M. call from the Judge, demanding to know what I'd done on the case so far. Maybe I could sell her on the idea that I'd come to the hayrack ride to check out the cars. We live by blind hope, don't we?

I wasn't sure how Mary would respond. This was a date, not a stakeout.

But she said, "Good. I'll help you."

"You will?"

"Sure. I'll take the cars on the far side of the barn. You take the cars on this side."

"You really don't have to do this."

"God, McCain, *please* quit treating me like a little kid, all right?"

"All right."

"When I don't want to do something, I'll

tell you. And I won't be subtle. I promise."

I should have been working for the Kinsey Report. I saw a lot of couples coupling in the backseats of their cars. High school kids, mostly. I moved quietly as possible. They were too enraptured to hear me. But I heard them: sighs, gasps, cries of pleasure, and a symphony of car springs. What could be lovelier on a Indian-summer night with a full harvest moon?

I even stopped to admire a few of the street rods. Chopped, channeled, louvered. They looked like something out of hot-rod magazines. Only in a small town like this could their owners feel safe leaving them and going inside. That was my dream. Have a wife and a couple of kids and pack them all in the front seat of a customized '39 Ford Phaeton and cruise up and down dusty Main Street on some fine June afternoon. Maybe I'd even give Judge Whitney a ride someday.

I didn't have much luck with taillights. The only one I found missing belonged to a '48 Buick, and I could see that the intact one didn't resembled the pieces I had.

I was just walking back to the front of the barn when I saw Mary, breathless, running up to me. "I think I may've found the car.

But it's just pulling out."

We ran around the side of the barn. It had been parked far to the west, out where a windbreak of oaks had been planted.

We finally got close enough to see the shape of the car: the unmistakable configuration of the '55 Chevy, which is, to me, one of the most elegant car designs ever built. From this angle, I couldn't see the taillight. The Chevy was moving without headlights along the back row of cars. It could pick up the edge of the graveled drive there and angle right out onto the county road that ran past the stables. I couldn't see the driver.

We kept pace with it by trotting to the county road.

Not until it got to the clearing between driveway and road did I see the taillight. It was raw yellow, two small naked bulbs. No red plastic covering.

I don't think the driver saw us. All of a sudden the car fishtailed through the gravel and shot onto the county road. It was doing 30 by then and 50 by the time it disappeared behind the trees.

"You get the license number?"

"I did." She gave it to me. "Illinois."

"Yeah. Good work."

"Thanks. Now what?"

"Need to check out the number."

"And how do we do that?"

"I noticed you said *we*."

She laughed. "I thought I was being sneaky." Then: "I want to help you on this, McCain. Susan was my friend."

"I'll call my buddy when we get back to my place."

"Is that where we're going?"

"If it's all right with you."

"It's fine by me."

We were silent on the drive back, listening to the Saturday Night Top Ten countdown on the radio. I think we both knew it was going to happen tonight. Though I still felt as if I were taking advantage of her, I decided she was right. I wasn't coercing her in any way. She knew I was in love with Pamela. I'd been honest with her, and that's all I could do. She sat very close to me and it felt good, felt right somehow. I was relaxed with her in a way I could never be with Pamela.

The lights were off downstairs. Mrs. Goldman was still out on her date. I would get a full report later. I'd become her father in all this. From now on I'd be shaking hands and approving her dates before I let her go out with them. Or was that being too strict in this modern age?

We went upstairs. I got the lights on and the heat turned up. Frost was on the grass.

She used the bathroom first. Did some more fixing up. Was lovelier than ever.

The buddy I'd referred to was a Chicago police commander who'd picked up his law degree at Iowa. He spent three years working for a Chicago law firm and found himself bored. He became a cop. We kept in vague touch. I'd never asked him for a favor before. He was married with two kids. I assumed he'd be home. Most married couples don't go out much, even on Saturday nights.

While I was in the bathroom brushing my teeth and slapping on more Old Spice, the phone rang.

Mary answered it and started talking. Asking questions. I couldn't get a lot of the exact words but I sure got the exact tone. Urgent. Scared.

She knocked on the door. "McCain?"

I opened the door. "What's up?"

"That was my mom. My dad's taken a turn for the worse. I really need to get home."

"Sure. Are they taking him to the hospital?"

"The doctor's coming to the house."

★ ★ ★

Even at night the houses in the Knoll look pretty rough. The Travers house was one of the best kept, thanks to Mary.

As I pulled up to the drive, I said, "I'll say prayers for him."

She looked surprised. "You still say prayers?"

"Sure."

"You still go to mass?"

"Sometimes."

"What's that mean?"

I shrugged. "Rarely."

She smiled sadly. "That's what I figured." She looked anxiously at the lighted living room window. "I need to get in there."

"I know."

She turned back to me. Lovely. Terrified of what might be going on with her father. "I would've done it tonight, McCain."

"Me too."

"I want it to happen." She leaned forward and gave me a quick kiss. "I'll talk to you tomorrow."

The drive back home was kind of melancholy. The suddenly cold weather gave all the houses an air of being battened down. Snug and cozy. Leaves tore from branches in the wind and crawled like small colorful

91

monsters across the grass and street. Spindly TV antennas swayed dangerously.

I parked in back and went up the private entrance stairs to my apartment. The door wasn't open more than an inch before something told me somebody was in there: the scent of expensive pipe tobacco.

I stood in the doorway.

"Don't turn on the light," he said.

"I don't usually take orders from burglars."

He sighed. "I'd appreciate it if you wouldn't turn on the light."

"And why would that be?"

"I don't want Cliffie to know I'm here."

"You call him Cliffie too?"

"Yeah. Behind his back I do."

I went in. Kitchenette, as it's called, bathroom, and bedroom on the right. The rest of the apartment is living room. He sat in the overstuffed chair across the room. I banged my knee on the coffee table.

"One good thing," he said, "you don't have to worry about hurting this furniture. It's been hurt all it can be."

"Part-time lawyer, part-time interior decorator. What an odd combination of jobs," I said.

"How do you know who I am?"

I took my coat off and draped it across the

rocking chair I'd inherited from Grandfather. "Number one, there aren't that many major assholes in town. And, two, I recognized your voice from court."

"Am I supposed to be impressed?"

"No," I said, lighting a Lucky in the gloom. "What you're supposed to be is afraid I may call Cliffie and have him book you for B and E."

"I came to talk."

"In the dark."

"Yes. In the dark. Cliffie would never understand."

I took a drag of my Lucky. "You want a beer?"

"I'm not much of a beer drinker. I work with my brains, not my hands."

"Good. That just means more for me."

When I opened the refrigerator door, the interior light shone on him. He was a dashing devil, David Squires, quite the country gentleman in his British tweeds and London riding boots. His expensive pipe tobacco smelled good.

"Please close that door. I told you I don't want Cliffie to know I'm here."

I closed the door. "Where'd you park?"

"Several blocks away. I took the alleys over here." I sat down and tapped the top of the Falstaff can with the church key. The beer opened with a *whoosh,* spattering foam on my hand. "You that scared of him?"

"He and his father run this town. I know you and the Judge think she still has some power. But she doesn't. Not the kind of power the Sykeses have, anyway."

"You came over here for what reason?"

"To hire you."

"Hire me? What the hell're you talking about?"

"I want you to find out who killed my wife."

"Cliffie's the law in this town."

"Cliffie's an idiot."

"That's not a very nice thing for his lawyer to say."

"Look, you prick, my wife's been murdered and I want to find out who killed her. Do you think it was easy for me to come here?"

"I suppose not."

"Then knock off the smart talk."

I sighed. "The Judge'll never go for this."

"These are extraordinary circumstances."

"So were all the times you gave your opinion of her in the newspaper."

There'd been a couple of articles in the past few years about *juris prudens* Black River Falls style. As the former District Attorney and now the town's most prominent attorney, Squires had had a good deal to say about "incompetent judges." He didn't name names. He didn't have to. Everybody knew he meant Judge Whitney.

"Maybe you killed her, Squires."

"Maybe I did. If you're half as good as you seem to be, you'll find that out and they'll hang me."

"There're a lot of other private investigators in the state. Good ones."

"None who know the town the way you do. You know Chalmers, too."

"Chalmers?" He was the ex-con I'd seen at the dance tonight. "What's he got to do with anything?"

"I was the prosecutor who sent him up. His lawyer convinced him I held back evidence and had a grudge against him. He wrote me a few letters from prison."

I lit one Lucky off another. Exhaled. Sat back. "Why the hell'd you jump all over the Judge and me this afternoon?"

"How many times do I have to remind you, McCain? My wife is dead. I walked in, and I saw you two standing there talking to Cliffie —" He sighed. "I needed to take it out on somebody and you two were elected, I guess."

I noticed he didn't apologize. Nelson Rockefeller had recently said his parents told him, "Never apologize, never explain." Apparently my guest lived by the same code.

"God, I don't know, Squires. This is pretty confusing. Maybe you should talk to the Judge yourself."

"Oh, and she'd give me such a fair hearing, wouldn't she? I wouldn't get two words out before she kicked me out of her chambers."

"I guess you're right about that."

"I need help, McCain. You know how hard it was for me to come over here and grovel."

Grovel? If this guy thought he was groveling, I'd have to invite him to watch me in action with the steely-eyed snob who was Judge Esme Whitney.

"I'll talk to her."

He stood up. "I really appreciate it."

"Since you seem to prefer the dark, how do I get ahold of you? You got a Bat signal you shine in the sky or anything?"

"What the hell is that supposed to mean?"

"Never mind."

Now I knew at least *two* things he didn't go in for: apologizing when he was wrong and reading Batman. It wasn't going to be easy working with this guy.

"Call me at my office. Say your name is Frank Daly."

"Frank Daly."

"I worked on his case when I was a prosecutor in Chicago."

"Nail him?"

"He got the chair. I had the pleasure of watching."

I almost asked if he knew Elmer the executioner at the tavern. They could compare notes on killing people. But I knew for a fact that Elmer was a Batman reader so I wasn't sure how they'd get along.

He moved skillfully through the shadows to the back door. "I'll wait for your call."

"This is crazy."

"So is my wife being dead."

The priest said, "Even though this is highly irregular, I did get a call from the Pope ten minutes ago and he gave us permission to go ahead with the ceremony."

I was beaming. All over. Head to toe, rosy glow.

"Now if you'll step forward," the priest said.

We stepped forward.

It was kind of crowded on the small altar.

The priest looked at his prayer book and then said, "Do you, Mary, take McCain to be your lawful wedded husband?"

"Oh, yes!" she said, looking lovely in her wedding finery.

"And do you Pamela take McCain to be your lawful wedded husband?"

"Yeah, I guess so," she said, after the teeny-tiniest hesitation. She, too, looked beautiful in *her* wedding finery.

"Good, then, my children. I now pronounce you man and wives."

I was just getting to the good part — the sleeping arrangements for our wedding night — when the phone rang.

" 'Lo."

"McCain?"

"I think so."

"This is no time to be a wise guy. I'm very, very nervous."

"Who is this?"

"Linda. Linda Granger."

"Oh, God, Linda, I'm sorry. I didn't mean to be a smart-ass."

"It's OK, McCain, that's how I expect you to be."

Which wasn't necessarily a compliment.

"I was wondering if you'd seen Jeff."

"Yesterday afternoon at Elmer's."

"How was he doing?"

I sat up on the side of the bed. Found my Luckies. Had my cigarette hack and then thrust a butt, as Mike Hammer likes to call them, between my lips.

98

"Is something wrong, Linda?"

"They can't find him."

"Who can't?"

"His parents. He didn't come home last night."

"Oh."

"How was he when *you* saw him?"

"His parents didn't tell you?"

"Tell me what?"

"He was pretty zotzed. I drove him home from Elmer's."

"Oh, God."

"He must've gone out and started in again."

Silence. "I suppose he told you."

"He said he wasn't sure you'd be getting married."

"That's all he said?"

"Yes."

"Nothing about me?"

"Nothing."

"Honest?"

"Honest."

"He may try and contact you, McCain. Please call me right away if you hear from him." She said something else but it was lost in her tears. She broke the connection.

It rained all day Sunday.

I ate two bowls of Cheerios for breakfast

and then read the funnies — I still like just about all of them, including *Nancy and Sluggo*, having, when I was a tot, a crazed crush on Aunt Fritzie — and then I listened to the local Top Ten while I did the exercises I'd learned in the National Guard.

The Top Ten is a little different out here. Whenever I'm in Chicago on a Sunday morning, I listen to their Top Ten and the sponsors are products like gum and cigarettes and pop. Out here, the sponsors are cattle feed, farm implement stores, and — my favorite — an ointment for cattle warts.

In the afternoon, I did some work. I tried to get Chalmers's number from information. None was listed. I also called Mary a couple of times. I wanted to see if she could steer me to a few close friends of Susan Squires. But she sounded so distraught over the state of her father's health — the family doc was there each time I called — that I didn't feel good about asking her for information.

I also kept trying the morgue. While the county coroner, Doc Novotny, has a somewhat suspicious diploma — "You are a proud graduat of Thayer Medinomics College" declares his degree, and no, that's not a typo; they really did leave off the *e* in *graduate* — he's a pretty helpful guy. (And just what the hell does "Medinomics" mean anyway?)

He's Cliffie's first cousin. I think he secretly resents the power his kin have. Somehow his own family was not dealt a fair hand at the table. So he helps me on the sly.

Except today. There was no answer until 4:00 P.M., when the rain was slashing down and I was getting ready for my Sunday evening dose of *Maverick*, two hours away. And then he said, "I'm sort of busy right now."

"With the Squires autopsy?"

"That seems like a hell of lot for car insurance."

I know code when I hear it. I don't read Shell Scott for nothing.

"Somebody's there, right?"

"Seems to be the case."

"Cliffie?"

"Looks like it to me."

"I'll try you later."

"See if you can do better on those rates, will you?"

And he hung up.

I managed to stay in my robe all day. Didn't even shave. Watched *Maverick*. Laid down to read a detective paperback and woke up at 6:30 A.M. I turned on the radio to a commercial advertising a popular polka band, Six Fat Dutchmen. They'd be in our fair city next week. One night only.

Six

One of the largest group of Negro settlers came to Iowa in the late 1890s. Representatives of a coal company that was having troubles with its white workers went south and made job-hungry blacks a lot of promises, a surprising number of which they actually kept. *Come to Iowa and prosper* was their message. By 1910, a couple of different areas of Iowa became Negro mining towns.

I remembered this from my history lessons when, on Monday morning, I went over to Keys Ford-Lincoln to see if anybody had been working late on Friday night before the Edsel premiere. A still-nervous Dick sent me back to the noise and energy of the service garage, where a man named Frank Kelton was working on a 1955 Ford station wagon. Like most other men, he had a lot of family pictures thumbtacked to the wall of his personal bay. He also had a yellowing photo of a group of black miners just stepping out of a mine. One of the men, most prominent because of his height, looked a lot like Kelton.

"Frank?"

"Yeah?"

I could see his coveralls but not his head or hands. They were lost somewhere up under the car he had on the hoist.

"Wondered if I could talk to you. Dick said it'd be all right."

"You give me a minute?"

"Sure."

All those great smells. Fresh coffee. Cigarette smoke. Cold concrete floor. Oil. Grease. New tires. Hot engines. Cool engines. Exhaust. And the sounds of glas-paks backing off. And rock-and-roll radio, a little Bill Haley if you please. And jabber jabber jabber. Mechanics with customers. Customers with customers. Mechanics with mechanics. And out the doors a beautiful autumn morning. Azure-blue sky. Temperature in the high 50s. The scent of burning leaves. Hawks didn't soar across the sky on a day like this, they tap-danced.

"Dick said it would be all right," I said again.

He was about my size, my age. One difference. His left eye was glass and strayed a bit. He was also a Negro. "I'm pretty busy."

"I won't take much of your time. It's about Friday night."

"Oh. You a cop?"

"No. I work for Judge Whitney."

He grinned. "I was in Korea, man. We

coulda used her over there."

"She's pretty nice most of the time."

"Yeah? Who says so, Stalin?"

Car repairman today, *The Ed Sullivan Show* tomorrow.

"I told the cops everything I know."

"Which was?"

He shrugged. He was about to say something when another man in coveralls, this one carrying a clipboard, came over and said, "You handle a tune-up about three this afternoon?"

"Should be able to."

"Thanks."

"You were saying," I said.

He shrugged again. "Dick said he'd pay me double for overtime to make sure everything was working right for Edsel Day. All the electrical stuff, I mean. I'm kind of a half-assed electrician. I guess he figured if there *was* anything wrong I could fix it. So I put in four hours. Got done for the day here at four-thirty, drove home and had dinner with the wife and kids, and drove back. Punched in at six and punched out at ten. Everything was in good shape."

"You know the Edsel they found the body in?"

"You kiddin'?"

"You know where it was?"

"Yup. Right over there in the corner. Along with two others. I put them there myself at the end of the day."

"While you were here, did you hear the sound of a car slamming into the edge of the building?"

"No. But this is a big place and I was playing the radio pretty loud, or I might have been up front talking to Susan Squires."

"You tell Sykes all this?"

"I tried. He didn't seem much interested. He just wanted to know if I'd seen anybody dump the body in the Edsel. I wanted to say, Hey, man, I seen somebody do somethin' like that, you don't think I'd call you right on the spot?"

That sounded like Sykes, all right. Don't confuse me with the facts. Just let me use my Chief Suspects dartboard and I'll have this case wrapped up in no time.

"You take a look at something for me?"

"I'm really in kind of a hurry."

He'd probably been wondering what I had in the lunch sack I carried. I spread the pieces out on his workbench.

"Taillight," he said.

"Right. Make?"

"Chevrolet."

"Model?"

"Could be one of three or four. But it's a 'fifty-five."

"Easy to replace?"

"Very. At least usually. But GM's union has been threatening a strike. They started a slowdown a while back."

"How long to get a replacement?"

"Couple days."

"So the driver probably hasn't replaced it yet."

"Could have. But probably not. Even if it's in stock, it'll probably take till tomorrow before he'd have his car."

"What if he's a do-it-yourselfer?"

"Buy his own kit, you mean? Install it himself? If that were the case, he could have it on by now."

"If he used a service garage, would it probably be you?"

"Iowa City and Cedar Rapids aren't very far away."

"So there's nothing special about this taillight?"

"Just that it's broken."

I thanked him and started to walk out of the garage when I saw the Keyses. They were both nicely dressed, as usual, Keys in a tan two-piece, his wife in a russet-colored suit that hid some of her boxy shape.

"Anything new on the murder?" Dick asked.

"Afraid not."

"I just wish I hadn't gone home so early," Mrs. Keys said. "If I hadn't left at seven-thirty, maybe I could have scared him away. You know, with both Susan and me working in the showroom together."

He slid a commiserative arm around her. "*I'm* the one who should have been here. But there was so much last-minute stuff — I don't think I was here twenty minutes the whole night." He frowned. "Well, if you hear anything —"

"I'll call. Don't worry." I nodded good-bye to Mrs. Keys.

You can never be sure how Judge Whitney is going to react to a piece of news. One time I told her I'd misplaced a vital piece of evidence in one of her cases, and she poured me a drink of brandy and said we all made mistakes from time to time and why didn't I just sit down and relax. Another time I told her I was three minutes late for our meeting because my ragtop had had a flat tire, and she threw her brandy glass at me and said it was time I got rid of that "embarrassing juvenile car." You may get the impression that she likes to start meetings on time.

"How's her mood?" I asked Pamela Forrest when I walked into the office that fine fall Monday morning. Pamela was wearing a blue shift with a matching blue ribbon in her baby-blond hair.

"How was Custer's mood after the Little Big Horn?"

"That bad?"

"She said you didn't call her."

"I didn't have anything to tell her."

"She said that shouldn't be any excuse."

"Just wait till I tell her what David Squires wants. You'll be hearing her scream." Then: "Why are you smiling? Do you *like* seeing me in trouble with her?"

"Oh. Sorry. I was thinking about something else."

And I got jealous because the only time Pamela ever looked that radiantly happy was when there was good news on the Stu Grant front.

"Something happened with Stu, didn't it?"

"Not with Stu exactly."

"Huh?"

"With his wife."

"Oh."

"Been called away, poor thing. Needs to spend two months with her ailing gran, poor thing."

"Here's your chance," I said, unable to keep the sadness from my voice.

Her smile got even bigger. "That's what I was thinking."

Her intercom buzzed angrily. "Is that who I think it is out there?"

"Yes, Judge."

"Tell him to get in here right now!"

"Yes, Judge."

I just kept thinking of how shocked she was going to be when I told her Squires wanted to hire me. I also just kept thinking about Pamela and Stu together for two months.

The intercom clicked off.

I turned and started for the Judge's chambers. But before I could take a step, Pamela grabbed my hand. "I say prayers for you and Mary all the time. That you'll — you know — get together. Would you do that for me? Say prayers that Stu and I get together? I'm so scared, McCain, I really am. This may be the only real chance I ever have at him. Two months."

"I'll try."

I didn't know which I felt more miserable about at that particular moment, Pamela or facing the Judge.

She had her tall executive leather chair turned away from me. All I could see was the thick blue smoke from her Gauloise cigarette curling up toward the vaulted ceiling. With its mahogany wainscoting, small fireplace, leather furniture, and elegant framed Vermeer prints, the office was seminally intimidating. The Supreme Court couldn't look a whole lot plusher than this.

She didn't say anything for a few moments. Making me anxious was her second favorite sport. The first was tennis.

Finally: "Is the door closed?" Still facing away from me.

"Yes."

"Are you sitting down?"

"Yes."

"Are you afraid I'm going to explode and really tear into you?"

"Yes."

"Good."

Still facing away from me. More smoke from her Gauloise. More silence.

Then: "And have you found the murderer yet?"

The only reason I put up with this was because of the shock I was about to give her. It would be like dropping a bomb on her desk when I told her what David Squires had proposed.

"No."

"And what did you do all day yesterday?"

"Stayed home."

"And did what?"

"Thought about the case."

"All day you thought about the case?"

"Well, except for when I was reading the funnies."

"And what else?"

"Watching *Maverick*."

"And what else?"

"Reading that paperback."

"Are you ashamed of yourself?"

"Sort of."

She whirled around and glared at me. "Sort of?" Her cigarette in her right hand, her cut-glass brandy snifter in the other. *"Sort of?"*

As I've said many times before, she's a good-looking woman, the Judge. Handsome. Imposing. She had on a fashionably styled fawn wool suit and white blouse this morning. Her short hair framed her face perfectly. She was the kind of woman you saw in high-toned magazines, pushing a poodle down Park Avenue.

"Well, I did actually do some work." I told her what I'd done.

"And I'm supposed to be impressed?"

"It's better than nothing."

"Oh, *there's* a slashing self-justification. *Better than nothing.* Inspiring, McCain. Downright inspiring."

I wanted to slide this one right across the plate. Startle her with it. Make her wonder if she'd heard me right. I wanted to rattle her like she'd never been rattled before.

I said, fast, "David Squires wants to hire me."

She said, "I know. He called me last night."

She slid it right back. Startled me with it. Made me wonder if I'd heard her right. "What?"

"He said he decided it'd probably be better to speak to me directly."

"Great. Just great."

"You were hoping to surprise me with it, weren't you?"

"I guess."

"And here I was the one who surprised *you*. That's funny."

"Real funny."

"I told him you'd do it, McCain."

"What?"

"He and Cliffie are up to something, and I want to find out what."

"You think Cliffie's involved in this?"

"Of course. Don't you?"

That's when she got me with the first rubber band. She keeps a stash of them in her drawer. She makes a pistol of her hand, thumb and finger, and then lets me have it.

She's good. Annoyingly good. The rubber band hit my nose and fell into my lap.

"Nice to know I haven't lost my touch."

"Yeah. I'm thrilled."

"Try and be a little faster next time. It's no fun if I always win."

She exhaled a great deal of French blue smoke. "Find out what they're up to, McCain, and fast."

"Yes, ma'am."

This time, even though I ducked, her rubber band got me on the forehead.

A sip of brandy. A glance at the two-hundred-year-old Swiss clock. "I need to get ready for court, McCain. And you need to get ready to do what you should've done yesterday." She shook her head. "And I certainly wouldn't go around admitting that you still read the funny papers. My Lord, McCain. Presumably, you'd like to be a grown-up someday."

I made it all the way to the door. Then she did some showing off. Just as I started to open her door, one of her rubber bands landed on my shoulder.

"It's a good thing you're short, McCain. I don't think I could've pulled that off if you were normal-sized."

All the time I was reading *Nancy and Sluggo* yesterday morning, I should have figured that

Judge Whitney would pay me back for it, comments about my size being her specialty.

The beautiful Pamela was on the phone when I went out. She didn't get to ask me to pray for her and Stu again.

Seven

I try to keep the covers folded back so you can't see the illustration of Captain Video, the boldest man in outer space and the most popular science-fiction show on TV. Friend of mine at Woolworth's was closing out merchandise that didn't sell. Among those items was a box of forty-eight small spiral notebooks that fit nicely in my back pocket. Great for keeping notes during an investigation — as long as nobody saw the illustration with the Captain and his zap gun.

Before I left the courthouse parking lot, I wrote three names on the first page of my fresh notebook:

Mike Chalmers
Todd Jensen
Amy Squires

I'd stopped by the parole office in the courthouse and gotten Chalmers's address. He was living on an acreage where he worked part of a farm for a salary. Kepler, the parole officer, didn't seem to have much faith in the man. "You know what the first thing he did was when he got out a few years ago?"

"What?"

"Cruised David Squires's place."

"Squires tell you that?"

"Squires didn't have to. A cop did. He saw Chalmers out there several times and thought I should know about it. So I call Squires and warn him and I call Chalmers and try and scare him."

"He scare, did he?"

"You know Chalmers pretty well?"

"Pretty well."

"Well, then, whaddaya *you* think? You ever know anybody who could scare Chalmers?"

I put the top down. Figured if I had to work, I might as well enjoy it. I was sixteen again. It's funny how quickly you can get nostalgic. Here it was 1957 and I was looking back at 1952 as the Golden Age already. Senior year in high school. Somehow, it seemed a slower, gentler time. Beer parties at the sandpits. Dancing with Pamela on the boat that goes up and down the river all summer. Seeing my dad finally shake off the war. No more nightmares. No more depressions. The year 1952 was just about as perfect as a year could get.

I was sitting at a stoplight when the black

Ford convertible mysteriously appeared next to me. A beautiful blonde. Kim Novak. Head scarf. Shades. Radio blasting Buddy Holly. Revving the engine. Daring me to drag her. A smile that said we knew each other, disturbing without me understanding why. And then she was fishtailing and her tires were screaming and she was laying down a quarter block of rubber. And then she was gone.

The acreage was scruffy, overgrown with weeds. Wire fences falling. Bottles and cans and papers littering the front yard. Windows crisscrossed with tape. A chimney that was little more than a pile of bricks atop a shingle-bare roof.

From what I could see, Chalmers had himself what was essentially a tenant-farmer agreement. There were a lot of acres in the adjacent land given over to soybeans and even more given over to corn. In the distance along the horizon line you could see a new big blue silo, a new red barn, and a new white farmhouse. Whoever lived there was doing all right for himself. But he still had some back acres he wanted worked so he offered a subsistence wage and a faded frame two-story farmhouse and disintegrating outbuildings and told the tenant farmer, in this case Chalmers, to go to it. Miserable as the conditions were — I had the sense that there was electricity but no indoor plumbing, thus the outhouse in the back-yard — it still had to beat being in prison.

There was a rusty Ford pickup sitting at the end of the dirt drive. The house and the outbuildings looked even rougher close up, badly in need of washing and painting. A John Deere even older than the truck sat near the left-leaning barn. A sweet-faced border collie ran in sad useless circles before slowing down to take a look at me. All that frantic pointless energy.

I got out. The border collie came over and growled. I put out my hand. She licked my fingers. I smiled at her and patted her head. She looked old and dusty and lost, a kind of quiet doggy sadness that can break your heart.

I went to the back door. Knocked. No an-swer. I went to the side door. Knocked. No answer. I went to the front door. Knocked. And that's when the girl came out.

She was probably around twelve or thir-teen, slender, shoulder-length blond hair with a tiny blue plastic barrette in it. Her flowered dress had been washed a few dozen times too many. You noticed the eyes first, the animal sorrow, the animal fear. And then, as she came into the sunlight on the porch, you saw the metal brace on her leg.

She just looked at me. "He isn't here."

"Who isn't?"

"My dad."

"Mike Chalmers your dad?"

She nodded. "I'm Ellie."

"You know when he'll be back?"

"He's at work."

"Your mom around?"

"My mom's dead."

"I'm sorry."

"I'm not."

"That isn't what girls usually say when their moms are dead."

"Well, it's what I say, mister."

She was going to step back inside at any moment. Shut the door.

"You wouldn't happen to have an extra glass of water on hand, would you?"

"My dad said I shouldn't ever let anybody inside."

"I'll drink it on the porch."

"You wait here."

When she turned and started walking I felt terrible about asking her for water. Walking looked to be such a ponderous effort for her.

She brought back a glass that was a couple of notches this side of clean. Handed me the water. I thanked her. There was an ancient porch swing suspended on rusting chains. I went over and sat down. Pulled out my cigarettes.

She said, "I bum one of those offa you?"

"Wouldn't your dad get mad?"

"My dad lets me smoke."

"How old are you?"

"Fifteen."

I held my pack out to her. And made her walk again. She did what I'd hope she'd do. Sat down next to me in the swing. She took a cigarette and I put a match to it. She inhaled and wiggled into a comfortable spot. I pushed on the swing. It glided gently back and forth.

"He was in prison."

"Your dad?"

"Yeah."

"You ever go see him in there?"

"A couple of times. He cried whenever I had to leave. Just broke down and cried." She said this with no particular emotion.

"How come you hated your mom?"

"It don't matter. She's dead."

"It's just funny, that's all."

"What is?"

"A girl hating her mother."

Head back, eyes closed, exhaling smoke. Fetching nymphette profile. "I'd get scared to go to school and she'd call me a sissy and slap me and stuff."

"How come you were scared?"

"Oh, you know."

"I guess I don't."

She looked over at me with one eye. She was a skilled con artist. "Maybe if you gave me another cigarette I'd tell you."

"You're not done with that one."

"For later."

"Ah."

For the very first time, she smiled. "I like that."

"Like what?"

"That word. *Ah*. I like words sometimes. Maybe I'll start saying it."

I gave her another cigarette. She tucked it behind her ear.

"How come you want to know all this?"

"I work for Judge Whitney."

"She's the one that sentenced my daddy." Again, and curiously, without emotion.

We swung for a while. It was nice out here. Anytime I stay outdoors on a sunny day I decide to give up my law practice and move west to the mountains and live off snake meat and tree bark. It's a hell of an exhilarating feeling. But that's usually when the first mosquito sinks its stinger in me so deep you suspect it's drilling for oil. And that's

121

when I see the ants in the picnic basket and realize I'll have to go take a pee behind a tree, and then moving west suddenly doesn't sound so good.

She said, "It's on account of my leg."

"Oh?"

"That I'm afraid to go to school."

"Oh."

"Most kids try and be nice to you. But some kids make fun of you. And I always end up leaving early and coming home and crying. Dad says don't give 'em the satisfaction, but I can't help it. It hurts my feelings. I mean I didn't *ask* to get polio."

Polio used to be a scare word. In summers, moms were afraid to let their kids go into theaters and swimming pools and shopping centers. Dads got terrified when their little ones ran a fever for more than a day or showed any kind of sudden weakness. It was our Black Plague. At best you might lose the use of a limb. At worst you could spend the rest of your life in an iron lung. Early death would be a mercy. Thank God for Jonas Salk.

"The worst is when we have little dances in the afternoon."

I watched her jaw muscle work.

"Mrs. Grundy at school said she was sure I could do it. Dance, I mean. Slow-dance.

Not rock-and-roll. That if I did a slow dance I'd be fine. There's a girl on *American Bandstand* who does it all the time. She's got a brace just like mine. But I'm scared to."

"You're too pretty to sit on the sidelines."

"You really think I'm pretty?"

"I sure do."

"You can't really be pretty if you limp."

"You sure can."

"Really?"

"Absolutely."

"That's what Dad says too. But I know as soon as I get out there and start dancing, they'll start laughing at me. You know, kind of whispering and all."

"They laugh about me being short."

"They do?"

"You bet they do."

"Does it hurt your feelings?"

"Sometimes. Sometimes it just makes me mad."

"Yeah, it makes me mad sometimes too."

We swung some more.

"What happened to your real mom?"

"Cancer."

The phone rang inside. She got up and struggled to go get it. I pitched the water over the side of the porch and felt kind of dirty about it. She was such a nice kid and here I wouldn't drink out of her glass. It was like I was betraying her or something.

She came back and said, "The social worker's coming out. I guess I better pick up the house before she gets here."

"You like her?"

"Not much."

"How come?" I handed her the glass.

She shrugged beneath her faded dress. "She always asks too many questions."

"Like me?"

"Oh, you're all right," she said. Then: "I saw you."

"Saw me?"

"Phone's right by the window."

"Oh."

"Throw the water out. Dad says I should be more careful, the way I do the dishes. Mom, she used to get on me all the time too. She'd always wash her own dishes after I washed them. Said they were filthy." She looked inside. "I better get moving."

"I hope I didn't hurt your feelings. Throwing the water out."

She shrugged. "Stuff like that don't hurt my feelings. It's mostly stuff about my leg."

I gave her a little hug. Nothing that'd scare her. Just a quick little hug. Then I kissed the top of her head and went down the steps and drove away.

Eight

"Doc Novotny asked me if I was going to see you today."

"He did?" I said.

"Uh-huh. Told him you had a haircut scheduled at one."

"He say anything else?"

"Said he'd been trying to get ahold of you all morning. Said he wanted to talk to you. Said you should stop over to his office at the morgue this afternoon. Said he should be around till about five or so. Said you probably wanted to see him too."

Just the mention of the morgue filled my nostrils with the stink of death. The rot of flesh. The cold shadowy refrigerated room. I didn't want to go.

Bill and Phil's is the barber shop of choice in Black River Falls. All the important people go there. Bill cuts *their* hair. Bill has what the nuns used to call aspirations. He's been serving important people for so long, he's started thinking of himself as important too. He and his Irma didn't have any kids — in a town like this, there's a lot of speculation about whose fault exactly it was — and he inherited a couple of farms, which he promptly sold before the '53 recession, so he's doing pretty well for himself. He's the conservative of the pair. You can tell that by looking at the photos he's got up on his barber's mirror behind the pump chair: Joe McCarthy. John Foster Dulles. And the mayor of Little Rock, Arkansas, who wouldn't let Negro students into an all-white high school. There are also American flag decals, American Legion decals, America First decals.

Phil is the Democrat. His photos run to Jackie Robinson, FDR, and Adlai Stevenson. He's got lots of American flag decals too.

Whenever customers get bored waiting their turn for a chair, they bait one or the other of the barbers. It helps pass the time. And it's more fun than radio.

Take today.

Lem Fuller, of Fuller's Hardware, was reading a *Confidential* magazine he'd bought at the newsstand before he came over. He said to Phil, the Democrat, "You ever read this magazine?"

"Wanda wouldn't let me bring that trash into the house," Phil said, knowing he was being baited.

"Well, here's sure an interesting piece."

Here it comes, I thought. Lem was more of a reactionary than Bill, unimaginable as that was.

"That little colored fella? Sammy Davis, Jr.?"

"Uh-huh," Phil said, snipping away at my hair.

"Says here he dates white women exclusively. Won't even give a colored girl a tumble. How do you like that?"

"I sleep fine at night," Phil said, "No matter who Sammy Davis, Jr., is with."

"You sure don't want the coloreds messin' with white gals, do ya, Phil?"

"Oh, heck," Bill said, snipping away at his own customer. "Phil wouldn't care if old Sammy took out every white woman in America. Phil's all for integration, don't you know. Colored and white mixin' it up all the time."

"I never said that," Bill said. "I just said we should treat 'em better."

"Well, Sammy Davis, *he's* sure gettin' treated better, I'd say," Lem said. "White gals with their tits hangin' out of their dresses and holdin' his hand and everything. Them white gals probably don't even care he's got one of them glass eyes."

Phil winked at Lem. "Maybe he's got somethin' else that's glass."

127

Lem laughed and said, "You think, Bill? You think he's got a glass dick?"

"I hear somebody else's got a glass dick," Phil said. He named another colored singer. "I hear he's a queer."

"Two for the price of one," Lem said. "He's colored and he's a queer. Lord God a'mighty." But the whimsical tone stopped suddenly and he put the magazine down and his face hardened in a way I'd never seen before. It was like in *The Invasion of the Body Snatchers*, how when you became a pod person your face changed, too, to something not quite human. "I'll tell you one thing. I got two daughters. Two nice, clean *white* daughters. I ever catch a buck nigger around either one of my daughters he's a *dead* buck nigger, I'll tell you that much."

"Aw, hell," said Bill. "I know some nice colored folks, don't you, McCain?"

"Sure," I said. "Lem's dad, for one."

"I'm gonna shut your goddamn mouth one of these days, McCain," Lem said. We'd hated each other for a long time.

"That before or after you burn the cross on my lawn?"

"Now, now, boys," Bill said.

I guess Lem was doing me a favor. He'd made me actually *want* to go to the morgue.

Anywhere to get away from him.

I was about two blocks from the morgue when a police motorcycle, a big Indian with a windshield and chrome handle grips and chrome saddlebags and streamers half as long the bike itself, came right up over the curb and sent me flying and my briefcase skidding down the sidewalk.

Cliffie. Clifford Wilbur Skyes, Jr.

"Aw, gee, counselor, I'm sorry. Guess I didn't see you there."

I'd like to say he only hurt my pride. But he'd also given my left hip a hell of a jolt. "I can see how that'd happen, Cliffie. Clear sunny day like this one."

"I thought we had an agreement about that Cliffie stuff." He had his Glenn Ford duds on, and he was looking fierce the way only an overweight bully with little pig eyes and jagged teeth *can* look fierce.

"Long as you keep pushing me around the way you do, the Cliffie stays."

"Don't forget, counselor, I could throw your ass in jail."

"Yeah, and I want to hear your lawyer in front of the Iowa Supreme Court when he tells them that you threw me in jail because I called you Cliffie. They'll get a good laugh out of that one."

"Yeah, well, they won't be laughing when my lawyer says you obstructed justice."

"Cliffie learned a new term. I'm proud of you."

"You're messin' again, McCain. And that's one thing I won't abide this time, and that's messin' by McCain. And there ain't even a *reason* to mess in this one, McCain. Me and my deputies already figured out who the killer is."

"This should be good."

"That peckerhead Chalmers. He's got it in for Squires — Squires sent him up — so he killed Squires's wife." He grimaced suddenly and leaned forward on his Indian, his butt off the seat.

"What's wrong?"

"You ever get hemorrhoids?"

"Not so far."

"Usually use Vaseline. But I tried this stuff on TV. Like to set me on fire. Doc Baines says it's 'cause I'm worried all the time. You know, about little Kim."

He wouldn't even give you the satisfaction of letting you hate him 100 percent clean and pure. He had to mitigate your hatred by having a two-year-old daughter with water on the brain. He was corrupt, violent, stupid, and yet he suffered. I'd seen him in the park holding her one day on his knee. I saw a tenderness and love I wish I hadn't seen. Even bad guys have good sides. Sometimes that can get downright exasperating.

He set his ass back down on his seat and said, "You've been warned, counselor. This is our case and we're just about ready to wrap it up and we don't want no interference from you or the Judge. Understand?"

He got the motor gunning so loudly, he couldn't have heard me if I'd answered him.

He wheeled the bike off the sidewalk and accelerated down the street, mufflers roaring.

Rita said, "She was a beautiful girl."

When I was younger, I never appreciated older women. Rita Fahey is forty-something and what the paperback writers always call "lushly built." She also has a lovely face, and eyes you just can't keep from watching. Kind of green but then again kind of blue. She's Doc Novotny's secretary in the morgue. She keeps the rock-and-roll loud, as if its festive qualities push back the cold stench of the place.

"She sure was."

"You know her, McCain?"

"No. But Mary Travers did."

She yawned. I tried not to notice what her sweater did. She never wore them tight, but it didn't really matter. "Cliffie's moving in for the kill. Between us, I mean."

As Doc Novotny's cousin and tacit boss, Cliffie gets first dibs on all murder information. I have to give him one thing. Cliffie's great at finding the person who *looks* like the killer.

"Oh? Who?"

"Mike Chalmers."

"God."

"Cliffie laid it out for the doc this morning. You ask me, it was Amy Squires. I saw her slap Susan Squires one night in the face at the dance pavilion. Out in the parking lot. My husband and I were walking to our car. She was screaming she wanted Susan to let go of her husband."

"When was this?"

"Three–four years ago."

"Well, look who's here," Doc Novotny said. He has the air of a politician who resembles Humpty-Dumpty. He smokes cheap cigars, paints himself with aftershave, and wears a rug that looks like a badly injured forest creature. "Cliffie's favorite guy."

"Rita said you gave him all the information already," I said, in a joking tone. "We get the crumbs as usual."

"Are you kidding? How long was Cliffie

here, Rita?" He dragged a stray hand down his paunch, as if he were stroking a pet.

"Oh, five–six minutes."

"My cousin's got the attention span of a kindergartner. I started explaining things to him and he immediately started looking at his watch. He thinks he's got his murderer already; why bother him with facts?"

"Mike Chalmers?"

"Rita tol' ya, huh? But if he would've listened to what I said, he might've changed his mind."

"You got something interesting?"

"*Very* interesting."

"Good. Let's go."

The shadows. The cold. The stench. None of it had changed. We walked into a tiled room with body drawers on one wall and two operating tables in the center.

He showed me the body. The head wound was vicious. Susan had one of those quietly pretty faces that holds an erotic power for men who take the time to look closely, that kind of First Communion chastity crossed with a whispered suggestion of desire.

"She die instantly?"

"Maybe. Can't say for sure."

"Blunt trauma the cause of death?"

"Without question."

"Time of death?"

"Nine to eleven P.M. Friday night. Can't do any better than that. She had a nice little body on her. Never showed it off much."

I'd thought the same thing and felt guilty about it.

"Pretty open and closed?"

He nodded. "Except for the bruises."

"Bruises?"

He took out a Penlite and worked it up and down her body. The bruises were old but still violent, even as they were fading. Upper thighs. Ribs. Lower back.

"They're old bruises."

"Yeah," he said. "They are."

"They have any significance to her death?"

"Not directly. But they suggest that somebody beat her up pretty often. Somebody who knew what he was doing. These aren't the kind of bruises that show when you have clothes on. The amateur wife beater, he'll give the old lady a black eye or a busted nose or a split lip and everybody knows what's going on. But your more devious wife beater, he puts the hurt on her where it don't show. Her thighs?"

"Yeah."

"There's an iron burn."

"Iron?"

"Yeah. Like the old lady does her ironing with?"

"She was burned with an iron?"

"Yeah. And pretty bad too."

"You ever heard of that before?"

"Oh, sure. Job like mine, I've heard of *everything* before, McCain."

"So what you're saying is that her husband, David Squires, put all those bruises on her?"

"You said it," Doc Novotny said. "I didn't."

PART II

Nine

My kid sister, Ruthie, said to her friend Debbie, who was sitting on the living room floor in front of that great postatomic social icon, the TV console, "She shouldn't dance with that blond guy. She looks better when she dances with dark-haired guys."

"Yeah, like that cute Eye-talian," Debbie said.

"*Which* cute Italian?" Ruthie said. "There're a lot of them."

"The one who sort of looks like Paul Anka except his nose isn't as big."

"Paul's gonna get his nose fixed."

"Where'd you hear *that?*"

"Mom showed it to me. It was in the newspaper."

"I wonder if his singing'll be different. You know, when they whack off his nose that way and all."

"Personally, I wish he wouldn't get it fixed."

"It's pretty big, Ruthie."

"Yeah, but it's sort of cute." Then: "I'll ask my brother. Sam, do you think Paul Anka's nose is too big?"

I said, "His nose isn't. But his mouth is."

"I think he's a *good* singer," Ruthie said.

"I'll take Tony Bennett," I said.

"He's *old*," Ruthie said.

"Your brother's sure a wise ass clown," Debbie said.

"He sure is," Ruthie said, glaring at me. She was pretty, like Mom, slender and fair. A lot of awkward guys trooped to our door to ensnare her. But at sixteen she wasn't quite ready to get ensnared.

It was Monday at 3:47 P.M. on the prairies of America, and for teenagers that meant just one thing: *American Bandstand* with Dick Clark. And conversations just like this, teenage girls (and boys, if they'd admit it) pondering the fates of the various stars Clark was featuring on his show to lip-synch their latest records. The Platters and Frankie Lymon and Gene Vincent and people like that. Some of them lip-synched pretty well; standing in front of a gray curtain they almost looked as if they really *were* singing live. But most of them were pitiful, lagging behind the record or given to sudden vast melodramatic showbiz gestures. More important than lip-synching, however, were the questions burning in the minds of the girls watching at home. Who were they dating? Were they as lonely as the songs they sang? Would they ever consider dating a girl from a place like, say, Black River Falls, Iowa? What was their favorite color? What was their favorite dessert? Did they want to have kids of their own someday? Had they ever met James Dean? Were they ever going to be on *The Ed Sullivan Show*?

Bandstand hadn't been on the air long but it had gripped the teenage imagination like a scandal. Small-town kids got to see how big-city Philadelphia kids dressed and danced. They became celebrities in their own right, the kids who danced on the show every afternoon. Justine and Benny and Arlene and Carmen and Pat and Bob were just some of the more prominent names. And the girls at home liked to match them up. Decide who should go out with whom. It was a kind of soap opera, because one day Bob and Michelle would be a couple and the next day here was Michelle, that slattern, in the slow spotlight dance practically dry-humping Biff right on camera.

Every once in a while it was all right to miss mass on Sunday (as long as your folks didn't find out), but you could never (repeat) *never* miss *American Bandstand*.

★ ★ ★

The Great White Fisherman was just coming in from the back porch as I reached the kitchen. Dad had taken a week's vacation to spend every afternoon up on a leg of the Iowa River with his rod and reel. This afternoon, still in his waders, his fishing hat jangling with a variety of hooks and lures, he stood in the back porch doorway and held out two pretty pathetic walleyes to my mom. "Here you go, hon, we freeze these for dinner Saturday night."

Mom winked at me and said, "Your dad must be going on a diet if this is all he's going to eat."

"I'm surrounded by wiseasses," Dad said, in his best Job-like voice. Then he grinned and said, "And I love it."

Different types of men came back from the big war. There were the sad ones, often mentally disturbed, who spent their time in mental hospitals or seeing psychologists. There were the thrill seekers, who kept trying to duplicate, usually in illegal ways, the excitement that danger had given them. There were the petulant ones, who felt that Uncle Sam should forever be in their debt for what they'd done for the Stars and Stripes. And then there were the men like Dad — the majority — who were just happy to be alive and exultant about being back in the arms of their loved ones. Sure, Dad had almost been killed, and sure, he'd seen a lot of terrible things happen, but most of the time he just thanked the Lord he'd gotten home safely.

He got us a couple of Falstaffs from the refrigerator and plunked them down on the kitchen table, a little quick-moving guy like me. He sat down and said, "Those Ford boys should be shot."

"The Edsel?" I said.

"Damned right the Edsel."

"It's all he can talk about," Mom said. "He hates it almost as much as he hates Nixon."

"Don't get me started on Nixon."

"And here I was gonna buy you a pink-and-puce one," I said.

He laughed at me. "Give it to Liberace. He'd probably go for it."

"Now there's nothing wrong with Liberace," Mom said from the sink, where she was putting the dishes in the dishwasher.

Dad had eventually gotten a good job after a spate of low-paying ones, so Mom now not only had the status symbol of the new tract house, she also had the status symbol of the new dishwasher. She was cute about it. She'd have a guest in and instead of seating them in the living room she'd lead them directly to the kitchen and say, "This is our new dishwasher." I told her she should dress up like a tour guide and sell tickets.

"Liberace's a cultured man," Mom said now.

"That's what you call him, huh? Cultured?" Dad sighed. "Aw, hell, I don't mean to make fun of him. I feel sorry for him. You know, how people pick on him and all. He just makes me nervous. I can't help it."

That's a trait I inherited from Dad: feeling sorry for so many people. I guess because Dad was always so little and poor and awkward around people, he identifies with outsiders. I felt the same way about Liberace. I couldn't sit down and watch him — he drove me nuts — but I didn't like people making fun of him either.

"Don't forget it's a TV night, sweetheart," Dad said to Mom.

Mom laughed. "You and TV night."

And it *was* kind of funny. Bishop Sheen was always warning about how the family TV set was actually pulling the family apart. Instead of eating dinner at the table the way they used to, families now sat in front of their TV sets and ate. So Dad had made a deal with Mom. Two nights a week he got to eat in the living room and watch *Douglas Edwards with the News* on CBS. He got to use the TV tray he'd bought for himself *and* he got to eat a Swanson TV Dinner. Personally, I thought TV dinners tasted like cardboard a dog had left damp. But Dad was never so happy as when he was in his TV mode.

"Oh, Lord, I forgot," Mom said. She smiled at me. "I was going to make him a pot roast stewed in vegetables and potatoes. But he'd rather have a TV dinner. If you can believe that."

"Why don't we have the pot roast tomorrow night?" Dad said.

"All right," Mom said, "if you'll take me to that new Debbie Reynolds picture this weekend."

"You got yourself a deal," Dad said. Then, to me: "The one I'd be lookin' into is that young doctor she worked for."

"Todd Jensen?"

"Yeah. I was fishing out at the park one day and I saw the two of them arguing. I couldn't hear them but I saw him push her."

"When was this?"

"Three weeks ago or so."

Dad never kibitzes on legal stuff but he has no hesitation about kibitzing on matters of investigation. It was from him that I got my habit of reading Gold Medal original paperbacks. The way he figures it, he's read enough whodunits to qualify as a detective himself.

He shook his head. "Life is like that sometimes, though."

"Come again?"

"You know. Couples. She's going with this doc and everything seems to be fine and then all of a sudden she starts running around on the side with Squires. I don't know any of them personally, but she sure looked to be better off with that doc. The way Squires treats the little people, he's a hard one to stomach."

The little people. That's what he always called the working class. And that was how he always saw himself. Because I'm an attorney, I get invited to some of the more high-toned events around town. I invite my family whenever possible. Most of the time they don't go — they always have a graceful excuse — but when they do I see how deep their sense of inferiority runs. Mom with her J. C. Penney dress and sweet goofy flowered hat and Dad with his blue suit from Sears looking ill-at-ease with all the local gods, the mayor and his cronies and the country club crowd. I guess that's why I like John O'Hara.

He's one of the few American writers to understand our caste system in Iowa. It's heartbreaking to see how uncomfortable Mom and Dad are around people they consider their betters.

I took out my Captain Video notebook and wrote in a line about Todd Jensen shoving Susan Squires.

"That's some notebook," Mom said, laughing. "Aren't you a little old for it?"

"Got a deal on a bunch of them."

"Long as it's not Mickey Mouse, you'll be OK," Dad said.

Ruthie came in and took two bottles of Pepsi from the refrigerator. "Gee, I wish *Bandstand* was on for three hours," she said dreamily, and floated out.

"Hurry up!" Debbie called from the living room. "The spotlight dance is on!"

I probably should have laughed about this in a superior older-brother way, but the truth was, the more I was out in the world, the better my high school days looked to me. I hadn't been especially popular but I had my '38 Ford and my collection of science-fiction magazines with Ray Bradbury stories in them. And I had that greatest luxury of all, time to call my own. I could hang around garages and watch mechanics work on cars; I could take in a double feature, a Randolph

Scott and a Robert Ryan if I were lucky; and I could sit in a booth at Rexall's and feast on a burger and fries while I read all the magazines I didn't plan on buying. When they make you grow up — or at least make you *pretend* to grow up — all that changes. Take my word for it.

"Kids today," Dad said.

"Yeah," I said. "Kids today."

"That Dick Clark is a con man if I've ever seen one."

My dad has a bullshit meter that is impeccable. I'd been thinking the same thing myself about Clark. Alan Freed goes to prison and his life is destroyed for a pittance in payola money. But somehow Clark remains untainted by the whole thing. It didn't make a lot of sense.

Mom said, "He looks like a very decent man to me. I was reading about him in *TV Guide* and they said he's a real family man."

That was all my mom needed to hear.

I spent another half hour at my parents' house. Mom cut me a big slice of pineapple upside-down cake, and while Ruthie was in the bathroom Debbie peeked her head in the kitchen and asked who I thought was a better singer, Tab Hunter or Sal Mineo, and then Dad said he was going to take a nap, and Mom joked that he'd need all his strength to chew through that TV dinner, and then I gave them both a kiss and left. I give Dad a kiss because I like to see him blush.

Family members.

Those are generally your first suspects in a homicide.

I learned that in my criminology courses, and it's stood me in good stead as an investigator. Family members frequently kill other family members, as the guys who wrote the Bible will tell you.

I'd already questioned David Squires, sort of, so now I needed to question his ex-wife, Amy. I called and she told me to come out only if I brought her a bottle of Chablis. She was having a small dinner party tonight and didn't feel like running into town and standing in line at the state liquor store.

I guess we're lucky. Some states are still dry. Iowa at least has liquor stores. Every time you buy a bottle of booze, they write your purchase down in a book. This serves two purposes: it allows the state to keep track of how much you're drinking, and it forces you to face your alcohol problem, if you've got one. Cotton Mather, I think, came up with this particular system.

The liquor store is usually busy, especially

when a holiday's coming up.

I got the Chablis in record time and drove out to the east edge of town.

You had to give Squires credit. He'd dumped his ex-wife, true, but he left her in good financial shape. The house was a split-level, a part stone, part wood, Southern California–style place with large stretches of sunlight-sparkling windows. Hard to sit around the living room in your underwear in *this* house, with or without your frosty can of Falstaff for company.

There were two cars in the sweeping driveway, a little red brand-new T-Bird and a dowdy green Chevrolet sedan.

The chimes were lengthy and pretentious, sounding vaguely like Gershwin. *Bob* Gershwin.

Amy'd put on a few pounds since I'd seen her last but they were not at all unbecoming. She'd been three years ahead of me in school. She'd always been beautiful, stylish. She had the sensuous mouth, the erotic overbite, the perfect classical nose, the brown-almost-ebon eyes that could be merry and sad at the same time. If her body was slightly overmuch, it was slightly overmuch in all the right ways. Dressed in a man's white shirt worn outside and a pair of jeans, she displayed two surprisingly small and very naked feet. She looked like the heroine of every Harry Whittington ADULTS ONLY paperback I'd ever read.

"Thanks," she said, and plucked the brown paper bag from my grasp. "You want some coffee?"

"I'd appreciate it."

As she led me through an impeccably modern and impeccably impersonal house, she said, "God, I think it's great."

"What's great?"

"That you think I killed that bitch."

"Yeah, there's nothing more fun than being accused of murder."

"Where that bitch is concerned, it's an honor."

We sat in a tiled kitchen, open and sunny, right out of a magazine. A huge island, shiny pots and pans suspended from above. White appliances — vast upright refrigerator-freezer, even vaster stove — and the pleasant scent of floor wax.

The coffee was made. We sat in the breakfast nook.

"How's the coffee?"

"Good."

"You don't have to lie, McCain. I know I make terrible coffee."

"OK, it stinks."

"Really?"

"Yeah. I mean, I'm sorry but it does."

"You want some sugar?"

"No, thanks. I'll just kind of sip at it."

"He always bitched about that too."

"Squires?"

"Uh-huh. Said I couldn't cook, said I weighed too much, and said I always made a fool of myself after two drinks."

"Sounds like a pretty good marriage to me."

"She was a conniver."

"That wasn't my impression."

"She took my husband, didn't she?"

"From the way you described your marriage, maybe he just handed himself over."

She sipped her coffee from a mug with a Republican Party cartoon elephant on it. "Maybe it's just because I'm used to it. But I think this stuff tastes pretty good."

I looked at her. "Happen to remember where you were Friday night between eight and twelve?"

She cackled. "God, you're *serious,* aren't you, McCain?"

"I'm afraid I am."

"I was right here. With my two little daughters, who never see their father because that bitch wouldn't let him come over here."

"How old're your daughters?"

"Nine and six."

"You talk to anybody on the phone?"

She thought a moment. "No."

"Anybody drop by?"

"No." Then: "I didn't kill her, McCain. Besides, they found her in a car trunk, right?"

"Right."

"I couldn't lift a person and throw her in a car trunk."

"She probably didn't weigh a hundred pounds."

"Oh, I see. I'm such a moose I could've done it, huh?"

"Just about anybody could've done it, Amy."

"You know what's funny?"

"What?"

"I was the one who got her on the cheerleading squad. I mean, she was nobody. And I just thought it'd be neat if I, you know, sort of extended my hand. I was the captain of the squad so I figured I should set the example. The other girls didn't want her. They called her 'Jane' because she was always reading those Jane Austen novels. My mom said Jane Austen was a lesbian."

"Well, if anybody would know about Jane Austen's sex life, it'd be your mom."

"But I felt sorry for her. So I insisted. And seven years later, she steals my husband.

Small world, huh?"

I tried the coffee again.

"Any better?"

"I'd just as soon keep my opinion to myself." Then: "People tell me you got into it with her in public a few times."

She shrugged. "It wasn't any big deal. I'd had a couple of drinks a couple of times. I mean she *did* after all steal my husband. Thanks to her my two little girls have no father."

"He left you pretty well provided for."

"Guilt. You run off with some little flat-chested Jane Austen type, the only way you can live with yourself is to lavish a lot of money on your ex and your daughters."

I waited a beat and then said, "He ever hit you?"

She waited several beats. "How'd you find out about that? That was one of the things I agreed to keep quiet about. In return for the house and the cars and everything."

"So he did hit you?"

"He wants to be governor, you know."

"So I hear."

"But first he needs to be state attorney general. The party fathers in Des Moines think he needs to be known better statewide before shooting for governor. So he'll run for AG first."

"And it'd look bad if the AG was an accused wife beater?"

She nodded. "The funny thing is, it was kind of sexy when it started out. I mean, he'd rough me up when we were making love, and at first I didn't mind it. He didn't really hurt me. Then he started losing interest in the sex and went right to the hitting. He knew just where to do it so it didn't show."

"He ever get carried away?"

"You mean like lose control?"

"Yeah."

"Once. Gave me a black eye and a split lip. I was really scared. I was going to talk to a shrink in Iowa City about it, but he begged me not to. Promised he'd never do it again. Right after that, he started seeing the slut — by my calculation, anyway."

"You ever hear about him hitting Susan?"

"No." She smiled impishly. "But I would've been happy to do it for him."

I looked at my Timex and I thought about whipping out my notebook. But then I decided Amy wasn't the sort of person you gave an edge to. She'd be gossiping about Captain Video for weeks. "I guess that's about it."

"Really?"

"Yeah."

155

"You know the crazy part?"

"What?"

"To make him jealous I started sleeping with a lot of his lawyer friends from Iowa City. And I made sure the word got back to him."

"And?"

She looked suddenly miserable, giving me a glimpse of the hard but fake exterior she'd constructed for herself. "I still love him, McCain."

"I'm sorry, Amy."

"This'll be our fourth Christmas without him."

She walked me to the front door. "I saw you at Rexall's the other day. Talking to Mary. When're you going to come to your senses and marry that girl?"

"I wish I knew," I said.

The half-hour drive to Cedar Rapids was pleasant. Fall is my season. The melancholy scent and the delicate beauty of the land, made all the more delicate by its brevity.

The office was on the west side of the river, above a corner grocery store that stank of rotting meat. The owner pointed me to the side of the stucco building and a flight of stairs that led to a door beyond which you could hear babies crying and adults coughing.

The nurse was pretty, much like Susan had been. Young Dr. Jensen's taste in women seemed to run to type. She said she was sorry but that since I hadn't phoned ahead for an appointment, I'd just have to wait my turn.

Babies always cry when they see me. I set three or four of them exploding just by sitting down. Mothers scowled at me for existing. What sort of telepathy or voodoo had I performed on their sweet little dears?

The people in the waiting room looked poor, that class below the working class that not even the war was able to help economically. I suspected that Jensen dealt with them because they were the only clientele he could get. But I had to give him his due for bringing help and comfort to people that most of society despises. In America, being poor is a sin if not a perversion.

Coughers coughed and sneezers sneezed, and a couple of old men hawked up enough phlegm to make me swear off eating for months. It was a swell way to spend seventy-three minutes.

I killed time by taking out my notebook and reading over what I'd written about the case so far. A couple of the mothers made faces when they saw Captain Video staring at them. One infant kept pointing at me and sobbing. I gave his mother my best "I'm sorry" look but she wasn't mollified.

I started looking my way through the magazines. The room was long and narrow, much like a boxcar, the cracked walls painted a mustard yellow. There were a lot of framed bromides about staying healthy, but they looked so old and decrepit they mocked their own wisdom. The chairs were mismatched, and so were the three tables upon which magazines were heaped. There were so many magazines, I got the impression that people were using this office as a dumping spot for periodicals they wanted to dispose of. Magazines of every kind: family, how-to, adventure, knitting, horseback riding, grain importing. And not a single one displaying cleavage. I found a *Collier's* with a John D. MacDonald novelette in it and read that.

He wore physician whites and a black serpentine stethoscope. His wild curly red hair was a lot longer than it should have been, and too many midnights had painted gray swaths beneath his green eyes. The equipment was sorely out of date, an examining room and two slender glass-fronted cabinets holding medicine.

He was busy with a clipboard when I walked in. He glanced up and said, "Just sit on the table. I'll be with you in a sec."

It was a couple hundred secs actually. Then he looked up at me and did a double-take Red Skelton would have considered hammy.

"You," he said, pure accusation.

"The one and only."

"You were at the dance the other night."

"Right."

"What the hell're you doing here?"

I took my notebook out from inside my sport jacket and held it up.

He gawked and looked as if he wanted to giggle. I'd forgotten to flap the cover back.

"Never mind the cover," I said. "This is where I keep my list of suspects."

"Oh, great," he said. "A cop with a Captain Video notebook —"

"I'm not a cop. I work for Judge Whitney of the District Court."

"That snooty bitch. What the hell's she got to do with any of this?"

"She wants to see justice done." I sounded like Broderick Crawford on *Highway Patrol*.

"I'll bet."

He walked over to the door and put a giant hand on the knob. "Get out."

"I have a witness who saw you arguing with Susan a few weeks ago. The witness says you gave her a very hard shove."

He didn't sound quite so sure of himself suddenly. "A shove is a long way from murder."

"It could be the first step *toward* murder."

His hand came away from the knob. He leaned against the east wall. "We had an argument was all."

"About what?"

He sighed. "I used to go out with her when she worked for Squires. Then she fell in love with him. And he ditched his wife and took up with her. But we never quite let it die, me 'n' her."

"*She* didn't let it die or *you* didn't?"

He hesitated. "Me, I guess."

"Everybody I know says she was still in love with Squires."

"She was. That's what we were arguing about."

"I'm not following you."

"She was still in love with him but he wasn't still in love with her."

"Oh? How do you know that?"

"I followed him several times."

"For what?"

"I thought maybe Susan would see him for what he was. You know, if I could prove he was running around on her."

"And was he?"

He snorted. "Hell, yes, he was."

"Anybody special?"

"Not that I could see. Just general nooky."

I took out a Lucky. He nodded to the pack and I gave him one too. When I got us fired up, I said, "You told Susan this."

"Yes."

"And she believed you?"

"Not at first. But she believed me after I showed her some pictures of him at a motel."

"You're a busy boy."

"I love her." He hesitated. "Loved her, I mean. And she loved me too. At one time. I look at that prick and I can't figure out what women see in him. He's the kind of guy who steals your woman just to prove he can do it. And then laughs in your face."

"He ever laugh in your face?"

"Once."

"When was that?"

"He saw me at an outdoor concert in Iowa City. He was with Susan. When she introduced us, he said, 'Oh, yes, the young man who's always calling you when I'm not home.' Then this big smirk."

"You know there's a possibility he beat her?"

"Possibility? Are you kidding? Of course I knew. I had to treat her a couple of times."

"She didn't want to leave him?"

"Leave him? Hell, she wanted to *help* him. It just brought out her maternal side. She talked about how his mother had been so cold to him. He didn't trust women. Deep down he was scared of them. She figured it was a small price to pay — taking a beating every once in a while — to help straighten him out."

"Been reading too much Freud."

"No shit," he said. "I hate all that crap. It was force-fed us in med school. And that's what I kept trying to tell her. That it didn't matter *why* he beat her — even if her Freudian psychology was right — what mattered was that he *did* beat her and that's all that counted. I told her he was going to get carried away some night and kill her. These things almost always escalate. He might not even *want* to kill her, I said. But he'd do it accidentally."

"How'd she respond?"

"The way she usually did. That I was just trying to come between them."

A knock. His nurse. "There's a call for you from Mercy Hospital, doctor. Emergency."

"Thank you." He walked over to a small sink, ran water, soaked his cigarette, and then pitched it in the ashtray. He turned back to me. "I don't dislike you quite as

162

much as I thought I would, McCain."

"Gee, that's good to know," I said.

I seem to make friends everywhere I go.

Ten

Rush hour in a town like ours means more milk trucks, more tractors, more hay balers, more combines, and more dump trucks. If you think traffic crawls in Chicago, you should spend three miles behind a plow-pulling tractor, watching its green John Deere ass wiggle and waggle all over the road.

I went straight to my rabbit warren of an office and called Judge Whitney with an update. She was gone for the day.

"Boy, she doesn't usually leave this early," I said to the beautiful Pamela.

"It's nearly four, McCain. That's not very early. She needed to go to Iowa City for some new shoes. She decided the ones she bought in Chicago aren't right for her dress after all."

"Sounds like a big do."

"It's Lenny."

"Lenny?"

"Lenny Bernstein. Or is it *-steen?*"

"Stein. And what's he got to do with it?"

"He's coming to the university, and he's invited her to have dinner with him afterward."

"Leonard *Bernstein* invited her to dinner?"

"Uh-huh. His secretary called yesterday to set it up. Then Lenny got on the phone himself and talked to her."

I've become immune to the Judge's name-dropping. A lot of the time I don't even believe she knows the people she claims to. But every once in a while, one of the names calls her and then I walk around in a state of disbelief for a couple of hours.

Dinner with Leonard Bernstein, no less. Lenny.

Plenty of bills, no money.

I sat at my little desk with my little Captain Video notebook trying to work out my finances for the next month. I drew two lines down the center of the page. Debits and credits. Just the way Mr. Carstairs taught us in Business Math back in high school. I looked at the sorry figures. My car really needed a new pair of glas-paks, but t'wasn't to be this month. I took out my huge stamp that says

120 DAYS OVERDUE!!!
PLEASE DON'T MAKE ME
TURN THIS OVER TO A COLLECTION
AGENCY

and started stamping bills. I sat back and did

what I always did: added up my debits and credits. If everybody who owed me money paid me, I'd be in fine shape. But my clients were mostly one step above public defender level and the prospects of their paying me weren't great.

So the collection agency threat was a joke and everybody around town knew it. Pops Mason may once have been a mad dog of a bill collector, but now that he was in his mid-sixties, some of the cunning had gone out of his pursuits. He was blind in his left eye, had rheumatism, gout, and prostate problems, and he never drank fewer than four quarts of Hamm's per day. He still pinched ladies a lot too. I knew all about his medical problems because he talked about them constantly to anybody who'd listen. He also had a long spiel about not having had a decent erection since he was fifty-three, a fact he blamed largely on the fluoride in the water. It was his contention that the Communists had been foisting fluoride on us as a way of seeing that our population declined, thus making us ripe for a takeover.

The knock was timid.

"Come in."

She appeared first: Linda Granger, rangy brunette. Her face was a portrait of good clean freckled midwestern carnality.

Normally there was a big-kid grin, and the mischief in the blue eyes was lacerating in its promise of fun and frolic. She dressed well too. Her father was a Brit who'd been a pharmacist in Sussex before Adolf consulted his various astrologers and decided to start a world war. He worked here at the pharmacy until Old Man Reeves startled everybody by taking off for Vegas one night with the Widow Harper and getting hitched. The Reeveses now lived in LA, from which they dispatched a blizzard of postcards about celebrities they happened to see. They had a running battle about Robert Taylor. Old Man Reeves insisted that Mr. Taylor had false teeth; Widow Harper angrily disagreed.

Anyway, Linda's father took over the pharmacy ten years ago, redecorated it, hooked up with the Rexall chain, and proceeded to make himself a wealthy and prominent local citizen.

Today, Linda wore a tight green sweater, jeans, bobby socks, and cordovan penny loafers. That sparkle I always associated with her was gone. Her skin was pale, her eyes dulled, their rims red from crying.

Jeff Cronin looked even worse than he had when I fished him out of the booth at Elmer's Tap the other day and gave him a ride home: wrinkled white button-down shirt and blue trousers, two-day growth of beard, eyes that didn't seem to focus. One or both of them smelled of tavern.

"She's kinda loaded," he said.

"Look who's talking," she said.

"It was her idea to come over here, McCain, not mine."

"He doesn't give a damn about our marriage, McCain. I do. That's why I told him we should come."

I smiled. "I don't think I'm following this."

After I jumped up and took the box holding the lie detector off one of the client chairs, I had them sit down.

Cronin said, "You got a beer?"

"I usually keep a quart in my pocket but I wore the wrong suit today."

"I need a beer."

"You've had enough beer," she said. "Is this what it'll be like being married to you?"

"We're not *getting* married, remember? There's a little matter of you cheating on me." Cronin had a quick temper. He was sliding the ammunition in the chamber now.

She looked at me. Pleading. "Did he tell you why he isn't marrying me?"

"No. I guess he didn't."

"Go on, then, tell him."

"You want him to know so bad, *you* tell him."

"No, you. I want you to hear how ridiculous this sounds in 1957."

For the first time, Cronin looked uncomfortable. His gaze fell away.

"Go on," she said.

He said nothing.

She said, "I spent a long night with Chip O'Donlon once when Jeff and I were broken up."

"I see." Chip O'Donlon was a client of mine. Which didn't save him from being an obnoxious idiot. He was a disgrace to dreamboats around the world.

"They went all the way," Cronin said miserably.

"That's not true, at least I don't think it is."

"She doesn't remember. She sleeps with a guy and she doesn't even remember."

"I'm pretty sure I didn't, McCain. But I wanted to be honest with Jeff. I wanted him to know everything about me. You know?"

"Honest." Cronin scoffed. "Some honest. We break up a couple of days, and she screws Chip O'Donlon."

"It was a month we were broken up," she said, "and I'm seventy-five percent sure I *didn't* sleep with him."

"That leaves twenty-five percent," Cronin said. "And he's telling everybody he *did* sleep with her."

"Gee," she said, "a math whiz. And he figured it out all by his lonesome."

"So," I said, "the problem is that your feelings are hurt that she spent time with O'Donlon?" I tried to sound as if this wasn't a much bigger problem than having stubbed a toe. "I sure don't see any reason to call off a marriage because of that."

"That isn't the problem," Cronin said. He made a fist. The knuckles I'd noticed the other day had scabbed over but still looked pretty bad.

"Oh?"

"The problem is that if she *did* sleep with O'Donlon, then he nailed her before I did."

"What a great way to put it," Linda said. "He *nailed* me."

I said. "You mean that the night she spent with O'Donlon she was still —"

"— a virgin."

"Ah."

"Now you see the problem. She was a virgin the night she went up to his place." He turned to her and said, with genuine grief, "It's nothing personal, Linda. It's just I was raised to believe that a man should always marry a virgin."

"Maybe I should've lied to you."

"Yeah," he said, sounding miserable again. "Maybe you should've."

I did the only thing I could think of. I took out the pint of Old Grand Dad from the bottom drawer, set three paper cups on the desk, and poured us each a hard jolt.

Linda teared up drinking hers. Cronin coughed. I felt my sinuses drain. A drinker I'm not.

"I guess I don't know what you want me to do," I said to Linda.

"Talk to him."

"Cronin's stubborn."

"He's also stupid."

"Quit talking about me like I'm not here."

"I don't want to put you on the spot, McCain, but who do you agree with, him or me?"

"Thanks for not putting me on the spot."

"Well, *somebody* has to talk some sense into that thick head of his."

"I agree with you, Linda," I said.

"Thanks a lot," Cronin said.

"She was being honest with you, Cronin. She wanted to get your marriage off to a good start. And now you're punishing her for it."

"What if he nailed her?"

"Will you quit using that word?" she snapped.

I said, "Do you love Jeff?"

"Of course I do, McCain. You know that.

I'm crazy about him."

"Do you love her?"

"Yeah. The bitch."

"Oh, really nice," she said.

"You think we could try that again? Do you love her?"

"Yeah. Pretty much I do."

"Then you should get married and forget all about this."

His scabbed knuckles came toward me. It looked as if he were slowing a punch in slow motion. "I just want to hit something."

"That wouldn't do much good," she said.

"God, Cronin. Look at her. She's a wonderful girl and she loves you!"

"Yeah, well, people will know she's not a virgin when we get married. I don't have to tell you how the guys'll be laughing about that for the next twenty years."

"I really don't think I slept with him," she said. "I really don't."

"Well, there you go," I said. "She's really pretty sure she didn't. And anyway, whether she did or not isn't anybody else's business anyway."

"Damn right," she said. "You listen to him, Jeff. What he's saying makes sense. It isn't anybody else's business."

"Yeah, but *I'd* know," he said, thumping his chest. "In here. And if my folks ever

172

hear, they won't want me to marry her."

"You're kidding," I said.

"Oh, no," she said. "He's *not* kidding. His parents are just like that. His mother got me alone the other night and asked if I knew what to do on my wedding night. I mean, it was sweet and scary at the same time. If they hear that I'm only seventy-five percent sure I'm a virgin —"

"The wedding's off," Cronin said. He looked ready to go crazy. Straitjacket time.

And then he was on his feet and stomping across the small space of my office. Out the door. Down the steps.

She put her head down and wept. Her shoulders shook. Her breath came in hot gasps.

I wished I could hold my liquor. My dad and I are just too small to be good drinkers.

I pulled a chair up next to her and started patting her head and back and shoulders. I wasn't sure what else to do. She just kept sobbing. I started alternately rubbing and patting. And then she turned to me and put her wet face into my neck and said, "I'm not telling the truth, McCain."

"You're not?"

"I said I was seventy-five percent sure nothing happened? But I'm really only about fifty percent sure."

And took her sobbing up yet another notch.

Fifty percent was a long way down from seventy-five percent on the absolutely sure scale. A long way. But I guessed it didn't matter.

"He loves you."

"I know."

"And he wants to marry you."

"You sure?"

"I'm positive. Just look how miserable he is."

She lifted her head and looked at me. "I'm not sure I understand that one, McCain."

"If he didn't want to marry you, he wouldn't be miserable. Don't you see?"

"Yeah, I guess so."

"I'll talk with him tomorrow."

"And say what?"

"Tell him he's in danger of losing you."

"What if he doesn't care?"

"He cares; believe me, he cares."

"It's not fair. Women don't care if *men* are virgins. And I'm probably a virgin anyway."

"Yeah, I know. Fifty percent."

"Maybe sixty, then. If that sounds better."

"I wouldn't give him any more statistics, if I were you."

She threw her arms around me and held me tight. I liked her. And she smelled good to boot. "Can I ask you something?"

"Sure."

"What if you found out your fiancée wasn't a virgin?"

I thought of Pamela. "I'd marry her in a minute."

"God, it's just so unfair. My mom's as bad as his. All I ever got growing up was 'Nobody'll want you if you're not a virgin.' And even if Chip and I did do something, I only did it because I was drunk and mad at Jeff. Jeff was the one who broke up with me. He gave me my Eddie Fisher records back and everything."

Then I said, "He's waiting outside in the car."

"How do you know? Maybe he left me here."

"He didn't leave you. I can hear his car. He loves you."

"He hates me."

"Well, at the moment he hates you a little bit. But he loves you a lot more."

"You're deep, McCain. You know that? People always say that about you, how deep you are."

"Well, I try, God knows. Being deep isn't always easy."

I slipped from her arms to the door. He was sitting out in the station wagon that belonged to his father's gas station.

"He's out there waiting."

"I love him so much, McCain."

"I know you do. And he loves you."

She was at the door. Hugging me. "I really appreciate your talking to us."

"No problem. I enjoyed it."

A chaste little kiss on the cheek and then she was hurrying down the steps to the car.

I waved to them. Cronin didn't wave back. He just backed up the wagon before she'd quite had time to close her door.

I went inside and resumed my life's work of being deep, which isn't half as easy as you might think. Just ask Socrates.

Just before five, the phone rang.

"Hi, Sam. This is Miriam Travers."

"Hi, Miriam. How's Bill?"

"Oh, actually coming along a little better than the doctor thought he would. In so short a time, I mean."

"That's great."

"The reason I'm calling, Sam, is to ask if you've seen Mary."

"Isn't she working at Rexall?"

"It's her afternoon off."

"Oh."

"She said she was going to stop by your office and then come home. She said she had something important to tell you."

"Gee, no, I haven't seen her. Of course, I haven't been here all afternoon either."

"Well, if you do see her, please tell her I'll hold supper for her."

"I sure will, Miriam. And that's great news about Bill."

At the time, I didn't think anything of the call. A lot of times, Mary got in her old DeSoto and drove to Cedar Rapids or Iowa City to shop. Being almost twenty-three, she didn't feel any great need to tell her mother her plans.

A harmless shopping trip.

That was my first conjecture about her absence.

But it would prove to be very wrong.

Perfume. A glimpse of a candelit dining room. A Jerry Vale LP on the record player. Mrs. Goldman was up to something tonight.

Her door was open so I peeked in. I wanted to ask her if she'd seen who'd dropped off a letter for me. An unstamped letter.

She was looking mighty fine, Mrs. Goldman was, in a tan tailored suit, her dark hair swept up in a stunning Cyd Charisse hairdo.

"Wow."

She laughed. "Thank you, McCain."

"In fact, double wow."

"My optometrist friend is coming for dinner tonight."

"He doesn't stand a chance."

She smiled. "That's what I'm hoping."

"So your date Saturday night went well?"

"Very well. Except for a little guilt now and then. You know, as if I were betraying my husband by going out."

"You'll get over that."

"I suppose. But I'll never forget him." The smile this time was sad, remembering her husband. She changed the subject. "So what's up with you?"

I remembered the letter. "You see who dropped this off on the front porch?"

"Afraid not, McCain. I was downtown most of the afternoon."

"Oh. Well, I'll let you get back to setting the stage."

"I made peach pie. I'll save you a piece."

"Thanks."

Up in my apartment, I settled in with a beer and a cigarette. Early autumn dusk, the colors of the sky, the last birds of day filling the fiery trees with song and silence. Soon enough their winter trek south would begin. In the alley, a couple of kids were playing the last act of their cowboy movie for the day, a shootout in which one was the victor and the other got to ham up a slow death as he dropped to the ground. Far away you could see the lights of the football stadium. They were testing everything for the big game Friday night.

I sat in the easy chair with a Four Freshmen album on the hi-fi. As much as I like rock-and-roll, I also appreciate the simple beauty of the human voice.

I kept studying the envelope and the letter inside.

CHEVY '55: (312) 945-3260

That's all it said.

Who had left the letter for me? And why?

Cliffie was convinced that Mike Chalmers had killed Susan to avenge his prison sentence. But if the '55 Chevy figured in the killing, it would tend to exonerate Chalmers. He didn't own a '55 Chevy.

I was just about to dial the 312 number when the phone rang.

"Hi, Miriam," I said.

"There's still no word from Mary. I'm getting worried."

"Sounds like a shopping trip to me."

"Oh, Lord, I hope so."

"Tell you what. I've got to go out for a while. I'll look around at the places she usually goes."

"It's just not like her to do this. Especially with her father in his condition."

I hadn't thought of that. And when she said it, the first faint note of alarm sounded in my emergency system. It really *was* out of character for Mary to do something like this. She was a dutiful daughter.

"I'm sure it's fine, Miriam. There'll be some perfectly logical explanation. You'll see."

"I just keep thinking maybe she's been in an accident or something —"

Then the words from her previous call came back to me. How Mary'd had something important to tell me. Something about Susan's murder?

"You just relax, Miriam. You'll be seeing her very soon."

"Thanks, Sam. You're such a good boy."

I smiled fondly. Miriam Travers had been telling me that most of my life.

I tried the 312 number. Eighteen times I let it ring. No answer.

Eleven

I stopped seven different places, looking for Mary. In the course of my travels, I played two games of pinball, bought a copy of the new *Cavalier* magazine with a Mickey Spillane story in it, caught up on some gossip with three or four old high school classmates, had an ice-cream cone at one of our favorite places, and walked around in a ladies' dress shop feeling very self-conscious.

No Mary.

In Chicago — or even Des Moines — a person can easily lose herself. So many places to go. But in Black River Falls, if she was out tonight, I should've run into her.

No Mary.

This left two possibilities. That she was visiting somebody, tucked inside a private house or apartment, or something had happened to her. The former seemed unlikely. Because if she were visiting somebody, she'd have called her mom and told her so.

Leaving accident or foul play.

I wouldn't have been so concerned if she hadn't told her mother that she had something important to tell me. Mary wasn't

181

much for drama. If she said something was important, it was.

I was wheeling around downtown when I saw Chip O'Donlon swaggering down the street, glancing at his reflection in store windows. He was an Adonis, he was; just ask him. I'd inherited Chip as a client from his older brother, who was currently serving two-to-five for setting fire to a rival's garage, said rival having had the temerity to start dating the girl the brother had dumped six months earlier. I hadn't been all that sorry to see him go. He was Adonis senior and real hard to take.

Chip. Maybe it was the sunglasses at night. Maybe it was his always calling me Dads or Daddy-o. Maybe it was because the cheap bastard never paid me. Chip liked telling people he had "a lawyer" and they'd been "in court" that morning and maybe he'd get "sent up" and maybe he wouldn't. His offenses ran to speeding, drag racing, giving beer to minors, and using profane language on a public street: nothing that would get him sent to prison, nothing that would mess up his pretty face. But he enjoyed the bad-boy image.

I whipped up to the curb and said, "Get in."

"Hey, Daddy-o." And he gave me a jaunty little salute.

"You hear what I said? Get in."

He got in. He was wearing enough after-shave to make a stadium tear up. "You got a hot poker up your butt or something?"

"No, but you will if you don't pay me the money you owe me."

The girls say he looks like Tab Hunter. He dresses like him anyway, all the California cool clothes you can buy between here and "Chi-town," as he frequently refers to Chicago. "Hey, man, you know I'll pay you."

"When?"

"Soon."

"How soon is soon?"

"Real soon."

I sighed. Actually, I didn't expect ever to get my money from this dimwit. But I had an idea of how to resolve the trouble Jeff Cronin and Linda Granger were having. To do that, I had to talk him into something. "When're you going to get a job, Chip?"

"As soon as my unemployment runs out."

I sighed again for effect and said, "I've got an idea."

"I hope it's a short one, Dad. I've got to meet a chick in five minutes." He gave me the wink. "I screwed her right on her car hood last night. Right out in the park. How about that action, Jack?"

God only knew what he was saying about poor Linda. He was a bullshit artist, as I said. If he slept with even 30 percent of the girls he bragged about, I'd be surprised. "I've got this equipment in my office I need to try out."

"What kind of equipment?"

"Why don't we say you'll find out when you get there?"

"When would this be, Dad?"

He was lucky I *wasn't* his dad. "I'll have to call you to set it up."

"Will it hurt?"

"No."

"Can I *tell* people?"

"Tell people?"

"You know. Like what I'm doing and everything."

"Oh, sure." By the time he got done telling the story, he'd be a guinea pig involved in atomic radiation tests.

"And why would I do this?"

"Because you're such a nice kid, Chip."

He giggled. He had a high, annoying giggle. "Sure, Dad. Sure."

"And because I'll wipe out your bill."

"No shit?"

"No shit."

"The whole thing?"

"The whole thing."

"Cool," he said.

"Now get your ass out of my car."

"The whole thing," he said, as he was opening the door. "Wow."

I tried the pizza place out on the highway. Our little town had just discovered pizza last year, a few years after we discovered television, the reception here being lousy until Cedar Rapids stations went on the air in 1953. There'd been resistance to pizza at first. To a town in the middle of the farm belt, it seemed awfully exotic, even slightly suspicious. The first month, Luigi's Famous Genuine Italian Pizza hadn't done so well. "Luigi" was a classmate of mine named Don Henderson, and how genuine his pizza was could only be determined by his genuine Italian chef, Jeff O'Keefe, all freckled, pug-nosed, red-haired sixteen years of him.

Then our local basketball team made it to the state finals. They lost after two games but still, for a town our size, just going was a serious achievement, especially considering that our starting center had lost two fingers in his dad's combine a week before basketball season started. On the way back, fighting a blizzard, their bus broke down near Luigi's and the kids had no choice but to try that most exotic and suspicious of foods. They stuffed themselves, gorged themselves, made themselves sick. Never had they tasted better food. And over the next few days, anchovy missionaries, they spread the word throughout town. Don Henderson was in business at last.

No Mary.

Don hadn't seen her for a couple of weeks, in fact. In fact, he hadn't seen *me* for a couple of weeks. What's the matter? You don't like my pizza anymore? (I noticed he'd picked up a modest Italian accent somewhere along the way.)

Still no Mary.

I went back home. A nice new red-and-blue Buick was parked at the curb. Mrs. Goldman's gentleman caller. I imagined she was dazzling him.

I pulled my car in back and went up the rear steps. Or tried to. Somebody was blocking them.

At first, in the soft moonlight, I wasn't sure who it was. He wore a cotton-lined jacket, gray work pants, and heavy steel-toed work boots. With his collar up, and his eyes burning angrily out of the mask of shadows, he would have made a perfect cover villain on an old pulp magazine.

He said, "You talk to me a few minutes, McCain?"

"Sure, Mike. The steps here all right?"

"Fine."

I sat on the bottom step. He sat up a few higher. We both lit up cigarettes. It was chilly but good chilly. The cigarette tasted great. I felt guilty. Nothing should give me pleasure when Mary was missing. And she was definitely missing.

"I think he's gonna arrest me."

"Cliffie?"

"Yeah."

"You didn't kill her?"

"Hell, no, I didn't."

"Squires said you were bugging them."

"I was. It was stupid but I did it. Two–three times I parked out by his house and just sat there."

"Why?"

"Because the sonofabitch sent me up without givin' my public defender information that woulda cleared me."

"You couldn't appeal?"

"He destroyed the evidence."

A familiar story among ex-cons. Not only had they been framed, they'd been framed by a DA with an inexplicable hatred for them.

"Why would he do that?"

"I knocked up his sister."

"*What?*"

"Back in high school. Before your time. Forty-two. Me 'n' Helen used to sneak off. Her folks hated me. I got her pregnant. They tried to run me out of town but they couldn't. Soon as he got to be DA, he came after me. He waited till he had a good chance to get me. I wasn't in on that armed robbery. I'd been trying to stay out of trouble. I'd been in a lot of little scrapes but nothing big. A friend of mine stuck up a gas station one night and got caught. Squires made him a deal. He wouldn't serve much time if he swore I was driving the car. He served two years; I served nearly eight."

"You can prove this?"

"My friend died in the can. Somebody cut his throat."

I believed him. There were all sorts of reasons not to — you'd naturally resent the man who put you away for eight years — but the simple way he told it seemed authentic. No anger, no bitterness.

I also had another thought. Maybe Squires had hired me just so I'd keep him apprised of everything I learned. Cliffie would bumble around for weeks and not find the right man. But Squires might have figured I might uncover something. He'd want to know everything if he was going to frame Chalmers. It was the only rational reason Squires would ever have come to me for help. Nothing else made sense.

"What happened to Helen?"

"Married a doctor. Lives in downstate Illinois."

"What happened to the baby?"

"Abortion. Her old man knew a doc in LA." He took a deep drag on the cigarette. "Funny. Couple of times she sent me a postcard in the can. On the date she had the baby cut out of her. Said she still thought about me sometimes. And the kid. She's a nice gal. Nothing like the rest of her family."

"You think Squires knew about the cards she sent?"

"Probably not."

"So he just wants to frame you for old times' sake?"

"I smacked him around pretty hard one day."

"When was this?"

"His office. When he was questioning me about the stickup. I lost my temper and went for him. Took a couple of guys to pull me off him."

Humiliation was something a man like Squires would never forget.

"What happens to Ellie if Cliffie arrests you?"

He shook his head. Looked up at the clear, starry night. In the distance you could hear the high school marching band practicing for homecoming weekend.

"That's what I'm scared of."

"You want a lawyer, right?"

"Right."

"You've got one. Cliffie makes a move on you, call me." I dug out one of the cards I always carry. "Day or night."

"I'll do my best to pay you."

"Don't worry about it," I said. Squires was using me and I resented it. Paying him back would be pay aplenty.

"I still have dreams about Helen."

"Apparently she still has dreams about you too."

"Two people who should be together, and somehow it never happens."

I tried not to think of the beautiful Pamela. Especially with Mary missing.

"Call me if you need me."

"I really appreciate this, McCain."

Upstairs, I phoned Squires at home. No answer. I tried his office. No answer. Then I decided to give Judge Whitney the satisfaction of telling her she was right.

Brahms was loud in the background when her man Andrew picked up. He has an accent. Some think it's British. Some think it's German. I think it's strictly Warner Brothers. He's from St. Louis, for God's sake.

She said, in her brandied evening voice, "I hope you're working hard."

"Very hard."

"Good. Then I can enjoy my loafing."

"I just called to say you were right about Squires."

I brought her up to date.

"Looks to me as if he wanted to learn everything a competent cop would find out about the murder. He didn't want anything to get in the way of his framing Chalmers."

"You don't have any doubts about Chalmers's story?"

"Not really."

"Now don't take offense, McCain, but I know how you people from the Knolls stick together."

"Not any more than you country-club people do."

"I don't know what you've got against country clubs. It's a good thing I know you like money. Otherwise I might start suspecting you were a Red."

"I think he's telling the truth."

"Once Cliffie arrests him, you may have a hard time convincing anybody about Squires's part in all this." A pause. I could hear her sipping, then taking a deep drag on her Gauloise.

"Have you considered the possibility that Squires is more than an opportunist?" I asked.

"Meaning what?"

"Well, one way we could look at this is that he's simply taking advantage of a situation he didn't have anything to do with. Somebody murdered his wife; on the spur of the moment, Squires decides to frame your friend Chalmers."

"On the other hand —"

"On the other hand, of course, Squires is behind the whole thing. He killed his wife and had Chalmers all ready to go as chief suspect."

"That's how you see it?"

"Maybe he was tired of Susan. Maybe she wouldn't let him out of the marriage — or threatened a scandal if she left him. He'd beaten her up pretty badly several times. A guy with political ambitions sure wouldn't want that kind of thing out and about."

"But Squires seems so unlikely —"

"Now you're going country-club on me. Just because he gets a manicure doesn't mean he's not a killer."

"By the way, I noticed that Lenny

Bernstein *doesn't* have manicured nails. Isn't that strange?"

"Very. Isn't that the eleventh commandment: Thou shalt have manicured nails?"

"On the other hand, he's most courtly and devastatingly handsome."

"How nice for the two of you. Can we get back to the murder now?"

"I thought you just might be interested when somebody of Lenny's stature pays a visit to this cow pie of a state."

"Why don't you share that metaphor with the Chamber of Commerce? I'm sure they'd love it."

Another gulp of brandy. "So, before you get any more tiresome, McCain, what do you propose to do next?"

"I propose to find Mary."

I told her about Mary's strange absence.

"She's a beautiful and intelligent girl. I'm sure she's fine."

God only knew what that meant, but it was getting late and the brandy was flowing freely. "I'm going to try and find Squires too."

"Why?"

"So I can resign. I don't want to be part of his charade anymore."

"That seems like a sensible idea. Good night, McCain. Just as long as we catch the real murderer before Cliffie does, that's all that matters."

I started to say good night but she'd already hung up.

Twelve

The next two days were frantic. There was no word about Mary. And I kept calling the Illinois number about the '55 Chevy. No answer.

One of Cliffie's third cousins had run into a manure wagon and had twice failed to appear for his scheduled court appearance before Judge Whitney. She found this intolerable. I spent most of the following forty-eight hours hunting down Bud "Pug" Sykes. He worked as a county assessor and had long displayed an affection for the bottle. I'm sure he was hiding out. This was between Cliffie and the Judge. Pug was incidental.

I found him the next county over. He was sitting through a western double feature with Al "Lash" La Rue and Monte Hale. I'd never cared for these gentlemen. "Lash" was a little too ornate for me; Monte, I'm sorry to say, always looked a little dense. Pug had been kind enough to park out in front of the theater, making it easy for me to see his license plate.

On the drive back, he said, "I got t'get me one of them whips. Like that Lash La Rue."

He was holding up family tradition: food stains on his work jacket, shirt, and trousers, and a dab of mustard on one cheek.

"I can see where that'd come in handy. A bullwhip like that."

"Bet cousin Cliff'd like one too."

I was so used to people calling him Cliffie, Cliff sounded strange.

"Cliff told me I didn't have to go to that there hearing unless I wanted to," he said. "And I didn't want to."

"You're in violation of the law, Pug. You *have* to show up. You be nice to the Judge, and she'll be nice to you."

Pug snorted. "Cliff always says, 'I wouldn't screw that old bitch with your dick, Pug.'" He giggled. "That Cliff."

"Yeah," I said. "A million laughs."

He was still giggling. "Hell, who needs Jackie Gleason when you got Cliff around?"

As soon as I dropped Pug off at Judge Whitney's office, I went straight to Mary's house. The street was sunny and lazy in another Indian summer afternoon. A small girl in pigtails rode a rusty old tricycle furiously up the cracked sidewalk. Then she stopped. She wanted to watch me walk up to the Traverses' door. She could have been Mary or Pamela fifteen years earlier, that smart little face, that clean but mended dress. The good ones in the Knoll never gave in to the temptation to go around dirty. Maybe they had little money and even less hope, but by God they were clean.

Miriam Travers had gotten old before her time. Life hadn't been easy. She'd lost a brother in the big war and a son in Korea, and now her husband had serious heart problems and her daughter was missing. The face was still pretty, the body still slender, but there was a defeated air about her, like a village that has been sacked by a particularly brutal army.

"Did you find her?" For just that moment, with hope in her lovely gray eyes, the hair was girlishly dark once more and the faded housedress a stylish frock. Miriam Travers was a young woman again, and life ahead looking happy.

"I'm afraid not, Miriam."

She hadn't said hello or invited me in. She'd just burst out with her hopeful question before I could speak or move. And now there was a death in her, one of those deaths you experience every time a phone rings and you plead with God that the news will be good.

She collapsed into my arms. There's no other way to express it. She didn't put her arms around me, she just fell forward. I held her. I didn't try to move her back into the house. I simply held her. She smelled of coffee and a faint perfume. She didn't cry or tremble or even move much. She was trying to hide. She needed to put her face deep into a darkness where she could not be reached by any more bad news.

Then Bill Travers was behind her, a wraith in a robe. He'd been a ruddy and robust man just a few months ago. The heart attack had taken both qualities from him. He'd lost at least forty pounds and moved uncertainly, like a bad actor playing a withered old man. His loose slippers slapped the floor and a bronchial-sounding cough filled his throat.

He slid his arms around her, and she turned with great sudden grace inside his embrace. And then she began crying. Sobbing.

"I'd like to go up to Mary's room," I said to the pale man impersonating Bill Travers.

He nodded. By the time I reached the narrow staircase, he was leading his wife carefully to the couch.

Time travel.

I remembered the day. Who didn't? V-J Day. End of the long and murderous war. Dad coming home. Six hundred *thousand* dads coming home.

There were Mary and I in the army caps our fathers had sent us, tiny American flags in our mitts, grinning at the camera. We had our arms over each other's shoulders.

There were other photos of the two of us: dances, bonfires, horseback rides, hot afternoons at the public swimming pool; later on, hot afternoons at the sandpits, high school beer cans glinting off the sunlight.

And Mary evolved in each one. More and more beautiful and graceful. A cutup, to be sure — clowning in a sport coat of her father's as a ten-year-old me watched; smoking a cigarette at her thirteenth birthday party (a very sophisticated lady until, as Miriam had predicted, she rushed to the john and threw up), me looking gawky and dumb in the background, shorter even than most of the girls; Mary in a talent contest lip-synching (as I recall) to "Music! Music! Music!" by Teresa Brewer, dressed up in a tux and top hat — and yet always with those wise and sober blue eyes. The Knolls and its despair and its violence had taught her, as it had taught too many of us, things we shouldn't have known at such tender ages, things that marked us forever.

Time travel.

I sat on the bedspread in the pink room, looking at the pennants and dolls and silly carnival gifts she collected over the years, at the desk where she'd done her straight-A work at the bookcase jammed both with classics and the occasional John D. Mac-Donald or Peter Rabe I'd given her. The room was scented with sachet and sunshine and memories. The autumn leaves brushed the open window. I could reach out and pluck one, like taking a plume of fire. I walked over to the desk and started going through the drawers.

I found it under a stack of papers: an envelope from the Dearborn County Courthouse, Dearborn, Iowa. It was a number-ten white business envelope with a window. The window was empty. I had no idea to whom it had originally been addressed. The postmark read December 2, 1955. Nearly two years ago. I turned it over. I recognized Mary's handwriting immediately. She had learned the Palmer Method well.

328-6382
Susan

I stayed a few more minutes, found nothing more. I stood in the doorway, overwhelmed with her, no thoughts of anybody but her.

I went downstairs.

"I put Bill back to bed. He shouldn't have

gotten up in the first place. It was my fault for carrying on the way I did. I'm sorry."

Miriam sat on the edge of the couch. I sat down next to her. Slid my arm around her.

"You ever see this before?" I showed her the envelope.

"No. Where'd you find it?"

"Mary's room. She ever tell you about writing the Dearborn Courthouse for anything?"

"Not that I remember."

I put it back in my pocket.

"You think it means something?"

"Probably not. But it's the only thing I found I couldn't explain."

She gave me a kiss on the cheek. "You're such a good boy, Sam."

"And you're a good woman, Miriam."

"If anybody can find her, I know it'll be you."

"Oh, I'll find her all right, Miriam," I said.

"I'll just keep saying prayers. I want to light some candles as soon as I can."

I gave her a squeeze and stood up. She started to stand too. "No need. I'll be fine." I walked to the door. "I saw that V-J Day photo up there."

She smiled. "You kids were so cute."

"That was a happy day."

"I still think of it," she said, "whenever I

need a little cheering up." Then: "But we were so naïve back then. I remember your mom and I talking about how all our troubles were over. You know, after the war, nothing would ever seem like much trouble at all." Then: "I didn't figure on Bud being killed."

It was a sad, defeated house now. I needed to get out of there.

Thirteen

I spent an hour and a half in my office the next morning calling every friend of Mary's I could remember. Then I spoke to the two women she worked with at Rexall. No help whatsoever.

In an effort to calm myself, I took the lie detector out of its box, dragged a small coffee table over by my desk, and set it up. Or tried to. I spent a full hour working with it. I got the ON button to glow red. That was about it. You know how in the movies that metal arm is always making jagged lines on the printout paper? The damned thing wouldn't budge for me.

What I was doing was killing time. Waiting for the magic hour of 11:45 A.M. I'd made a call earlier and asked what time the boss man went to lunch.

The Rollins building is what passes for a skyscraper here. Four stories, ornate 1920s facing, right down to gargoyles perched on the corners of every floor.

Squires came out walking fast. There was always that briskness about him. Dapper as usual. Another dark blue suit, this one with pinstripes, gold collar pin, seawater-blue necktie, gray hair perfectly combed.

A sweet time for walking, so sunny, so filled with the pretty women of Black River Falls doing their shopping or pushing their strollers in the small stores that make up the downtown.

I fell into step next to him. "Hello, counselor."

"I've been waiting to hear from you."

"I've been busy."

"Oh? I hope that means you've come up with something."

"I sure have."

"Good. Let's hear it."

Other than his first unhappy glance at me, he'd stared straight ahead. It would be a pleasure to snap his head around and see his startled eyes.

"The news is that you killed your wife and you're trying to frame Mike Chalmers for it."

His head not only snapped around, he stopped walking. "What the hell're you talking about?" He spoke in a loud whisper.

"I was a little skeptical when you showed up at my place that night. A man like you could afford any investigator in the state. Why me? You told me the truth about one thing: because I know the territory. So I'd hear plenty of gossip. Hear if anything would get in the way of setting up Chalmers. Like a witness who saw *you* at the murder scene. I was like a minesweeper. And now you think you're in the clear. Thanks to all the crap you've been feeding Cliffie, he's more convinced than ever that Chalmers is his man. And he's going to arrest him very soon."

"Chalmers *is* his man."

"You're a jealous man, counselor. You like to keep your women locked away from everybody else. And when they disobey you, you like to beat them. Or maybe you beat them just for the fun of it."

"Do you realize I could sue you for slander for what you just said?"

"Care to try? And Mary Travers is missing. I think you may be behind that too."

"I'm firing you. Right here and right now."

"I'll send you a bill."

"After what you've just accused me of, do you honestly think I'd pay it?"

"No, I guess you wouldn't. But let me tell you something. I won't let you get away with it."

Cold smile. "You won't, huh?"

"No. I won't."

The smile stayed but now it turned nasty. "You think the Judge has the power to go up against Cliff when he makes up his mind?" I noticed he no longer called him Cliffie.

"It's happened before."

"Well, it won't happen this time. Chalmers is the man. No doubt about it. He had the motive, the method, and the means, as they taught us in law school. He's obsessed with me and has been ever since I put him behind bars, where he belongs."

"You framed him then too. Because of your sister."

His features froze. "I take it he's your client now?"

"He is."

"So he'll have ample opportunity to tell you a lot of lies about my poor sister. Did he also tell you that he raped her and that's how she became pregnant?"

"If he raped her, why didn't you charge him with it?"

"And put my own sister through a rape trial? I happen to love her very much."

"You think your sister would tell me that if I called her?"

"If you *do* call her, McCain, you'll be a very, very sorry man, believe me." He paused and then said, "My uncle owns the plant where your father works. And I'm my uncle's favorite nephew."

"I'll mention our conversation to the union rep at the plant."

"Not even a union man can save his job if I put the word in Don's ear."

I sighed. "Just when I think you couldn't get any more despicable, Squires, you manage to come up with something worse. You lie awake nights planning this stuff?"

"Yes." The cold smile again. "When I'm not busy planning world domination." He had a nice expensive watch and shot his cuff to peek at it. "My stomach tells me it's lunchtime."

"That's funny. *My* stomach tells me you make me sick."

I sat in a café and had a cup of coffee and a wedge of apple pie with a piece of cheddar on it. I smoked three Luckies. I plotted what I was going to do to our friend Squires. You know how you start thinking of all these neat ways of getting rid of somebody. Mussolini would have been proud of some of the things I thought up.

I was at a stoplight on my way to my office when the black Ford appeared. The mystery blonde in the black sunglasses looked more fetching than ever: white turtleneck, black silk head scarf, blood-red nail polish. That wry sexy smile. And that throbbing Chuck Berry music.

The light changed.

I floored it.

I shouldn't say *I* floored it, the entity in *control* of me floored it.

Here I was, this hardworking young attorney trying to be mature and respectable when this *being* took possession of my body and made it do all sorts of crazy and degrading things — like, drag racing.

I laid down twenty feet of black rubber.

I beat her to the next stoplight and waited for her to catch up.

This time, she discarded the smile. In its place was a pout. Pure Brigitte Bardot. She started jabbing the accelerator. Her glas-paks thundered. She was going to put me in my place.

My glas-paks roared back at her.

People on the corners stared at us: the red Ford; the black Ford. The erstwhile counselor-at-law; and the gorgeous girl.

About to put the pedal to the metal.

Red light . . .

Yellow light . . .

Green li—

Which was when Cliffie pulled into view on his big Indian motorcycle catercorner from us. Wouldn't he just love to give me a ticket so stiff it would let him yank my license for a year or two?

The black Ford sped away faster than was strictly wise, given Cliffie's hunger for ticketing people. He gave her the bad eye but didn't move.

She beat me to the next light and then disappeared again, turning an illegal right on red.

School was getting out. I sat there waiting for the grade-schoolers in the crosswalk. Their clothes were new. The school year was only a couple of weeks old. I remembered what it was like, buying school clothes in August, your folks taking you to the department store all worried about the money they'd barely been able to scrape together. Buy good clothes had been *my* folks' reasoning, they last longer. I always went for Buster Brown shoes as a tyke because of his dog Tige and Smilin' Ed McConnell on the radio. I also liked clothes that either looked Western — because of Roy and Gene — or futuristic — because of the *Flash Gordon* serials they ran over and over at the Rialto. The new-shoe smell was almost as good as the new-car smell. And the first few times I wore them, I treated my clothes with the deference shown toward something Christ

had personally blessed, careful of everything I ate and drank.

Then the crosswalk was empty.

This time, I didn't lay rubber. I drove
away like the nice respectable attorney I am.

I smelled him before I saw him.

I don't suppose that's a nice thing to say,
even about Cliffie, but it's true. There was
just this *odor,* a kind of generalized Cliffie
odor, wafting its way out the open window
and my office door.

I wondered how many other times he'd
broken into my office.

He had his cowboy-booted feet up on my
desk, his campaign hat pushed back on his
fat head, and a cigar butt stuffed into the
corner of his mouth. He wore his holster rig
complete with billy club.

"What the hell's that thing?" he said,
pointing to the sprawl of gear on the coffee
table.

"A lie detector. Something I'd like to get
you hooked up to sometime."

"I don't need no lie detector. I just look a
man straight in the eye. That's all I need."

"My hero," I said.

He said, "You got troubles, counselor."

"I do, huh?"

"You certainly do."

"Well, why don't you make yourself comfortable, Chief, and tell me about them."

"You thinkin' of suin' me or some other lawyer bullshit like that, you just forget about it. I'm the law and I got a perfect right to be here."

I nodded to the Pepsi bottle and piece of waxed paper on my desk. "You got a perfect right to drink my Pepsi and eat my sandwich?"

"That beef was a little tough."

"Gee, I'm sorry to hear that."

"You got to buy grade-A meat, counselor. Tastes a whole lot better than the gristle you been buyin'."

I sat down in one of the client chairs. "What the hell do you want, Cliffie?"

That sat him up straight as I knew it would. I was sick of his ugly self parked in my chair. He was all things slothful. "I thought we agreed you wasn't to call me that."

"When you break into my office, all bets're off."

He had his elbows planted hard onto the surface of my desk. "You just like to rile me, don't you, counselor?"

I sighed. "Get to it. What the hell're you doing here?"

"OK then," he said, and extracted from his lips the wet cigar butt. "You been botherin' a friend of mine."

"That being David Squires."

"Then you admit it?"

"I don't admit anything." Then: "He tell you he hired me?"

"What're you talkin' about? Why would Squires hire *you?*"

"Because he killed his wife. And he thought maybe he might have left a couple of loose ends. Maybe a witness, or something dropped at the scene of the crime. He knew you'd be too stupid to figure it out so he hired me."

"Bullshit. He arranged for me to get that Lawman of the Year award last year from the Skeet Shooters Association over to Fort Madison."

"He was kissing your ass, Cliffie. You can help him. If you couldn't, he wouldn't even speak to you."

Cliffie was angry and hurt and confused. "Well, you can bet your ass I'm gonna ask him about that. About him hirin' you."

He looked pretty bad just then, Cliffie did. Knowing you've been betrayed will do that to a person. Just saps all your strength and focus. He said, like a kid, "He really hired you?"

Somehow I couldn't take any more pleasure from hurting him. "It wasn't anything really big."

"I mean, you don't get Lawman of the Year award unless them fellas really think you're doin' your job."

"I expect not."

Then, trying to regain some dignity, he said, "But Chalmers was the one what killed her, that Squires girl."

I shook my head. "I don't think so. I don't have proof yet, but I think I will have pretty soon. So before you arrest Chalmers, I'd appreciate it if you'd call me first."

He stood up. Rage had replaced hurt in those dog-brown dog-stupid eyes of his. "We'll see how Mr. Fancy Squires likes it next time he wants a favor done and stupid ol' me tells him no."

"That's right. You've got to stand up for yourself."

"Just because I ain't educated."

"Right."

"And just because I ain't pretty like him."

"Right."

"And just because I got this here skin condition and can't bathe often as I should."

"Right."

"And just because people think the only reason I got this job is because my old man runs the town."

"Right."

"Well, I'll show Mr. Fancy."

"Damn right you will, Cliff. Damn right you will."

For just a moment there, I almost felt sorry for him. I almost forgot about the many times he'd billy-clubbed me and punched me and kicked me, just in the line of duty as he saw it, and the many times he'd cheated and railroaded and framed my clients. For a moment, I forgave him all of it. And then, being Cliffie, he had to go and disabuse me of my Christian charity.

"Chalmers is the man, McCain."

"He didn't have any reason to kill her."

"He hates Squires."

"Who doesn't?"

"Well, I guess that's a good point. But he's also an ex-con."

"So that automatically makes him the killer?"

"McCain, I've read a lot about ex-cons. Hell, let's face it, my family's got a lot of ex-cons in it. Our family reunion looks like a prison yard."

He walked to the door.

"I'm gonna be one busy boy, McCain. First I'm gonna meet up with our friend Squires and tell him what I think of him; then I'm gonna go arrest Chalmers. You can take that as fair warning."

A minute later, he fired up his Indian and was gone.

The phone rang a few minutes later. Dick Keys.

"Any word on Mary yet?"

"Not yet, Dick. Thanks for asking."

"She's sure a sweetheart. You give her folks my best."

"I sure will."

Hesitation. "I'm kind've embarrassed about somethin', McCain."

"Oh? What's that?"

"I've got this employee, Merle Ramsadle? He served a little time for taking a car a few years ago, but I hired him here as a mechanic and he's been a real good employee."

"I'm glad to hear it." What was he getting at?

"He was here Friday night, too, and he saw somethin', and he shoulda stepped up to the plate before this. But you know how it is when you're out on parole. You don't want to get involved in anything you don't have to."

"What'd he see?"

"I'll let *him* tell you. He's standin' right here." Then he said, "Just tell him what you told me, Merle, and everything'll be fine."

"I didn't have anything to do with that killing, Mr. Keys."

"I know you didn't, Merle."

"People think just because you've been in prison —"

215

"Just talk to Mr. McCain, Merle. He's a nice young lawyer."

The phone was handed off and Merle Ramsdale said, "Hi, Mr. McCain."

"Hi, Merle. I really appreciate you doing this."

"I just don't want the parole office to think I had anything to do with the murder."

"I'm sure they won't, Merle. Just relax and tell me what you saw."

"Well, I stepped outside to have a cigarette. It was a nice night and I'd been puttin' in a lot of hours and I just thought some fresh air would do me good. And that's when I saw him, when I was outside having a smoke."

"Saw who?"

"The big guy."

"What'd he look like?"

"Well, as I said, a big guy. Like a basketball player. But heavier. Stronger."

"You notice anything else about him? Kind of clothes he was wearing?"

"Dark jacket of some kind. Zipper, I think. And dark pants. Nothing that really stood out."

"Anything else?"

"His hair. There was a whole lot of it. Curly."

"The color?"

"I think it was red. It was dark. He was over in the shadows. Back by the used cars."

"What'd he do when he saw you?"

"Just kind of ducked down between a couple of cars."

"What'd you do?"

"I shouted out, 'You want some help with somethin', mister?' I figured that'd chase him away."

"And did it?"

"Yeah. He took off running."

"You see him again?"

"Nope. But then I was inside until quittin' time."

"You didn't tell anybody about it?"

"Wasn't anybody around but me."

"The other mechanic?"

"He was on dinner break."

"How about Susan Squires?"

"Oh, she was there, but up front. Decorating the showroom. I didn't want to bother her."

"And you haven't told anybody about this till now?"

"Uh-uh. Like I said, I want to stay away from the cops as much as I can. It'd look funny, me involved in some kind of thing like this. I just got married. My wife wouldn't like it either. She won't like this, me talkin' to you. But it just kept stayin' on my mind. You know how things get some-times."

"Well, I appreciate this."

"I hope I've been helpful."

"You've been *very* helpful."

"I'll put Mr. Keys back on."

"Thanks again, Merle."

"Don't know if that was any help," Keys said, when he came back on, "but I thought you should know."

I thanked him and hung up.

So young Dr. Jensen had paid Susan a visit at the Ford dealership Friday night just before she was killed.

I wondered how he'd explain it.

I tried his number twice. Nothing. Then I tried the Illinois number and got no answer there either.

I wanted to go looking for Mary, but in the past two days I'd covered the entire town, talked to a good fifty people, followed up every lead and partial lead that'd been offered me. And nothing.

I spent half an hour trying to rig up the lie detector. It was like a Martian trying to plug in a Venusian appliance, to borrow a phrase from *Galactic Adventures*, one of the maga-zines I'd read as a kid.

I was just getting ready to go home for the

day when I decided to give the Illinois number another try.

A female voice said, "Carmichael residence."

"My name's McCain. I'm a lawyer in Black River Falls, Iowa."

"Oh, Lord."

"Ma'am?"

"This is about the taillight, isn't it?"

"Why, yes, ma'am, it is."

"I told Ronnie he should've made her turn it in."

"Ronnie being —"

"My son. He was over there visiting my sister."

"I see. And your sister is — ?"

"Amy Masters-Squires is her married name."

"You said, 'He should've made *her* turn it in.' She was driving the car?"

"Yes. She was having some kind of trouble with hers so she borrowed his."

"I see."

"You know about her ex-husband then?"

"Yes, I do."

"He was a peach. Any man tried to beat *me* up, I'd be out of there in two minutes flat."

"That's how she should have handled it."

"It sure is. I expect Ronnie back in an hour or so."

"I'll call later." I didn't want to tell her that she'd just told me the best part of her story: the ex-wife at the murder scene. "It may be tomorrow."

"If you see that sister of mine, tell her I'm thinking about it."

"I sure will. And thanks for your help."

"You bet."

A few minutes later, I was on my way home.

Fourteen

I've found that the true gourmet chef learns to mix and blend prime ingredients in new and interesting ways. All you need is a hot plate.

Take Dinty Moore Beef Stew and a small can of creamed corn: a rare delight. Or a can of Campbell's Mushroom Soup and a can of Foster's Small Potatoes: exquisite. Or a can of tuna fish and a can of tomatoes: Voilà! Two more rules: always serve everything with potato chips, and, if the main dish leaves something to be desired, douse liberally with ketchup. If ketchup can't kill an offending taste, then you've created a gourmet meal that God did not intend to *be* created.

Such are the ways of bachelorhood.

I was eating a tuna-and-tomato sandwich in the easy chair so I could watch TV when Tasha, Crystal, and Tess fanned out at my stockinged feet and looked up at me with imploring eyes, the effect of the tuna being not unlike that of, apparently, catnip. They rubbed me, they yowled at me, they head-butted me, they tail-switched me. I kept nodding in the direction of the bowls of kitty food I'd just set out for them. I reminded them that they didn't even technically *belong* to me (a local girl who'd gone to Hollywood had left them in my care), so any largesse on my part was all the more remarkable. They were unimpressed with my argument.

I had a headful of confusion. Squires was the most likely killer. But what had Todd Jensen and Amy Squires been doing at the murder scene?

I washed up, changed into a work shirt and chinos, and went out the door. Which was when the phone rang, and I had to go back inside.

"McCain?"

"Yeah." It was Cliffie.

"Guess where I am?"

"Where?"

"The Sixth Street elevator."

"Good for you."

"Meet me at the bottom as soon as you can."

"Any special reason?"

"Yeah. We're gonna take a ride."

"That sounds romantic."

"You won't be so smart when you get here."

"So I don't even get a hint, huh?"

"Just get your ass over here, counselor."

"See you in a bit." I'd run out of smart remarks.

The phone rang a moment after I hung up.

"One of my spies tells me that something's going on near the Sixth Street elevator."

"So I'm told by Cliffie."

"He's going to beat us, McCain."

"No, Judge, he's not."

"He'd bloody *better* not, McCain." Whenever she used the word *bloody,* I knew she was mad. She'd seen *The Bridge on the River Kwai* and had been using it for emphasis ever since.

The Sixth Street elevator is an inclined cable car that rises to the top of a four-hundred-foot hill. Seems sixty–seventy years ago, the then mayor had a brother-in-law who'd rigged up a similar elevator in Dubuque. Why not in Black River Falls? reasoned the mayor. The elevator is operational about sixty days a year. That's not because of the weather but because the damned thing doesn't *work* any more often than that.

There were three police cars and an ambulance sitting at the base of the hill. The cable car was parked at the bottom end of the tracks.

Cliffie hooked his thumbs in his Sam Browne and swaggered over to me. "I'd sure like to listen in on that conversation when you call the Judge."

"And why will I call the Judge?"

He just grinned. "C'mon, we'll take a ride."

The hill was thick forest except for the cable tracks. In the moonlight, the burnished autumn trees looked wan. A crowd was just now forming. I saw the town's most famous radio newsman, E.K.W. Horner — and don't ask me what E.K.W. stands for, nobody knows — with his bow tie and hand mike interviewing a young lawyer from the DA's office. It was a warm night and there were a lot of hand-holding couples. I wanted to be one of them. And I wanted the hand I was holding to be Mary's, sitting out at the A&W root beer stand, eating hot dogs, and watching the carhops show off on their skates. Some of them were pretty damned good. The girls appreciated them as much as the boys.

Cliffie escorted me to the cable car. You could see the various layers of paint the car had received over the years to cover up the dirty words kids put on there. The words got progressively dirtier. Back in the 1930s HOT DAMN! was a bold expression. We'd now worked our way up to SHOVE IT! God only knew what the future would bring.

The tiny car smelled of oil (from the cable overhead), cigarettes, cigars, perfume, and simple age. The wooden sides had been rained on one-too-many times, and now there was a creeping odor of mortality about them.

Cliffie took a childish delight in operating the elevator. He closed the door, took off the brake, and slammed the car into motion. I was knocked back against the wall.

"You know he didn't finish high school," Cliffie said, as we started crawling up the steep incline. All we could see, side to side, were the branches of fir trees that covered the hill.

"Who didn't?"

"Your client."

"I have a lot of clients."

"But only one killer, I'll bet."

I sighed. "Aw, shit. Is this about Chalmers?"

"It sure is, counselor."

"He didn't kill anybody."

"He didn't, huh? You know what I said about him not finishing high school?"

"Yeah."

"Well, that don't mean he's dumb."

"No, of course it doesn't."

"He managed to fool you." The lazy,

mean, hillbilly smirk. "And foolin' a coun-selor like you — well, you'd have to be a mighty smart man."

I still had no idea what he was talking about. As long as it wasn't about Mary. It ter-rified me that it was going to be about Mary.

The car continued to inch its way up the slope, slowly now that the incline was steep. I wanted to get out and push.

"I still don't get a clue?"

"You just keep your britches on, coun-selor." He pulled out a flashlight and beamed it through the window. He was looking for something next to the cable tracks. "Should be comin' up any time now."

I started watching the hillside outside the car and saw nothing remarkable. Ground covered with needles of fir and spruce. An occasional beer can, empty red package of Pall Malls, potato-chip bag, all pitched out by cable car passengers.

Cliffie was getting excited. He started smirking to himself, which was always a bad sign, and then he brought the car to a jerky halt.

"We're not there yet," I said.

"Oh, yes, we are."

"We're only halfway to the top."

"That's where your man put it."

"My man?"

"Chalmers."

"Ah."

"I hate that. That 'Ah' thing you say."

"I'll have to try and say it more often."

"Let's see you play smart-ass now, counselor."

He threw the doors open and stepped outside. The pine scent was powerful. The silver half-moon was vivid. It was a beautiful night. Cliffie led the way around the front of the car. Then I saw why he'd stopped. A big white *X* had been made on the dark ground with some sort of flour or powder.

"Who put that there?" I said.

"Guy who found it."

"Guy who found what?"

"You'll see, counselor. Don't worry."

He led us into the trees then, but not far. We didn't need to go far. The body of David Squires was waiting alongside the forest trail, sprawled on its back between two trees. The bark on one tree ran with a sickly looking sap.

Cliffie started to move forward but I grabbed him.

"What the hell you think you're doin', counselor? I'm the law around here."

"The crime scene. We could destroy evidence."

"That more of the stuff them Commies

taught you at Iowa?"

A few years ago, a professor of economics had written a mildly left-wing book about the poverty of migrant workers. Ever since then, the local McCarthyites had accused everyone on the faculty of being a Commie.

"*Crime scene*. You've never heard that expression before?"

"I just wanted you to see and then apologize."

"For what?"

"For accusing this fine man of being a murderer."

"A, he wasn't a fine man, and, B, I still think he had something to do with the murder of his wife."

I don't know what kind of reaction Cliffie'd expected from me — probably some kind of swooning admission that I'd been wrong about Squires — but I wasn't giving it to him.

I sighed. "I'm sorry he's dead."

There was a small hole on the right side of his forehead. I assumed this was the shot that killed him. His tan suit was grass-stained on the knees and elbows. His right cheek was bruised badly.

"You are, huh?"

"He was a human being."

"Not much of one, according to you."

"He beat his wives pretty badly. That isn't exactly an admirable trait."

"Some people just think their shit don't stink. That's what sticks in my craw."

"Meaning me?"

The smirk. "Yeah. Maybe."

"So what's the connection to Chalmers?"

"Two people seen him get on the cable car with Squires here."

"When was this?"

"About two hours ago."

"You going to tell me who they are?"

"The witnesses?"

"Yeah," I said.

"Oh, sure. I'll even let you interview them so you can twist their stories."

"He didn't do it."

"You sure of that?"

"I'm sure."

"What I'm sure of is, you're full of shit. You and the Judge."

"Gosh, and here I was going to invite you to my birthday party."

"C'mon, McCain, the bastard's nailed and you know it. He's an ex-con."

I had a lot of things to do.

"Let's go," I said. "I need to get back."

He looked at the body and then smirked at me. "Nailed good and tight."

★ ★ ★

I was just walking back to my car when the block-long Lincoln Continental swept up. Jeeves was driving. I called him Jeeves because of my fondness for P. G. Wodehouse. I also called him Jeeves because I had no idea what his name was. He was Judge Whitney's driver, that's all I knew. He rolled down the window. He was in livery. He looked proper and tough at the same time, not unlike the Judge herself. He nodded to the backseat.

I opened the back door and peeked in. Judge Whitney handed me a drink of some kind. "Get in."

I got in. Jeeves swept us away. The Lincoln was so cushy it was like floating. Beethoven was low on the radio. There was a heavy window between front and backseats. The Judge was dressed in a black suede car coat and slacks. Between us on the plump seat was a large thermos of whatever we were drinking.

She said, as we sailed along, "I've done something nice for you."

"Thank you. It actually tastes pretty good. For alcohol."

"It's called a Manhattan and that isn't what I had reference to."

"Oh."

"I was referring to David Squires."

"Some dirt?"

230

"A *lot* of dirt. He was broke."

"You're kidding. What happened to that inheritance of his?"

"Squandered on every kind of cockamamie idea you can think of. He had this business manager — an old family friend — in Chicago. The fellow basically figured out a way to embezzle a lot of money."

"When did Squires find this out?"

"A couple of years ago. As he was a member of a prestigious family, the local bankers kept everything quiet. He was deeply in debt. The bank was almost ready to foreclose on his estate."

"I take it you're getting this from a banker?"

"Of course."

"Nice to know they keep their secrets."

She clucked, something she rarely does. She curses, she rolls her eyes, she shakes her head, but she rarely clucks. "Secrets are confided upward, McCain. Since my family is *more* prominent than the Squires family, I have a right to know."

"I believe the English called it the Divine Right of Kings."

"You're perfectly happy being uncivilized, aren't you?"

"Downright delirious. Just give me a good Three Stooges movie and a box of popcorn and I'm in heaven."

She took a healthy swallow of her drink. "I just gave you some important information. Now *do* something with it."

"Any suggestions?"

"You're the investigator, McCain, not me."

"So you think his being broke had something to do with his murder?"

"Don't you?"

And with that, she got me. Her rubber band. Right on my little Irish nose.

"Don't people give you funny looks when they see you carrying rubber bands around?" I asked.

"People *never* give me funny looks. They wouldn't dare."

"I guess that's a good point."

This time, I ducked.

She lifted her phone. I heard it ring up front. Jeeves picked up. She said, "Take him back to his car" and hung up. "Cliffie could always get lucky, you know," she said. "You've got to wrap this up."

I stared out the window at my little town. It looked so cozy with night here, the lights on in all the friendly windows, the gray images of TV flashing through the air, so many contented people in those living rooms, old couples and middle-aged couples and young couples, babies waddling around in industrial-strength diapers and older brothers on the telephone nervously trying to impress the girl they just called. I loved the whole history of the town, way back to when the French explorers tried to take advantage of the Indians hereabouts, only to learn that the Indians were slyly taking advantage of *them*. I started thinking about Mary again, and I got scared. Two people were dead. Whoever had killed them probably wouldn't mind killing a third.

When we pulled up next to my Ford, the Judge said, "Time to get to work, McCain. *Serious* work."

Fifteen

When she opened the door I handed her the plastic bag.

"What's this?"

"What you left behind Friday night."

"It's a little late for games, McCain. Plus which, I'm in a rotten mood. I'm out of Chablis and my monthly visitor just dropped in tonight."

Somebody somewhere has probably compiled a list of all the synonyms for menstruation. Amy Squires was sticking with the most common one.

"So do I get invited inside?"

She smiled with that big ripe mouth of hers. "I only have two kinds of gentlemen callers. Those who bring me booze and those I want to sleep with. You don't have any booze and you look like you're about fifteen."

She knew how to stroke a guy's ego.

"So we just stand here?"

"So we just stand here."

She wore a black blouse and jeans. Bare feet. She looked sexy in the same sleepy, voluptuous way she usually did. Probably not a great wife but a hell of a mistress. She rat-

234

tled ice cubes in her glass.

"I thought you were out of Chablis."

"Chablis, yes. I didn't say anything about Scotch."

"Ah."

"You and your ahs. And just what the hell is this anyway?" She held up the plastic bag I'd handed her.

"You broke out a taillight Friday night at Keys's around nine-thirty, when you were trying to get away."

You always hope they'll break down in tears and confess, the way they do on those TV courtroom dramas. She got defiant. "You prick."

"You hated her and were jealous of her and you killed her."

"I'd think it'd be the other way around."

"What?"

"First, I'd be jealous of her and *then* I'd hate her and *then* I'd kill her."

"Thanks for the English lesson."

"I didn't kill her, McCain."

"Then can you explain what you were doing there?"

She sucked some ice into her mouth and talked around it. "Maybe I need a lawyer."

"Maybe you do."

"Too bad David is dead. I could've called him."

"I can see you're terribly bereaved."

"The bastard dumped me. Why should I be bereaved?"

I guess she had a point, though with two children between them, I'd think she'd want to put on a show for the girls.

"But you admit you went to Keys's?"

"Sure I admit it."

"Why?"

"To tell that bitch to have David pay me the alimony he owes me. Nearly five thousand dollars now. I'm supposed to go to Mexico on vacation next month. I need the money. He's also behind in child support. I never wanted kids anyway. We were young. I wanted to have fun. But he was always thinking of his political career. Election PR photographs. You know, the candidate with his two darling little daughters? We're both shitty parents. Neither of us actually wanted the girls. To be perfectly honest, I mean."

A house of love. The way kids pick up on things, I'm sure they'd long ago sensed the attitude she was describing.

"She was alive when you got there?"

"Very. She was hanging balloons in the showroom."

"And you had words?"

"She played the naïf as always. I guess men find that attractive. 'Behind in his payments? My David? I don't see how that could be.' That sort of bullshit. I started screaming at her."

"Did you strike her?"

"No."

"How did it end?"

"I just stormed out. That's one of the things I do well, storm out. I'm told there are a couple of other things I do well too."

"Want me to guess what they are?"

"I just wish you didn't looked so damned young, McCain. I'd get arrested for contributing to the delinquency of a minor."

"You make them show IDs at the door?"

She smiled that slow, sexy smile. "There are different kinds of ID, kiddo. If you catch my drift."

I wondered if she kept a photo of Mae West in her wallet.

"He was broke."

This seemed to surprise her. "Nobody was supposed to know that. The bank was floating him for a while."

"When was the last time you talked to him?"

"A few days ago. And I didn't talk. I screamed."

"The money?"

"Of course. I'm over him by now. All I want — want*ed* — from him was good old

Yankee greenbacks."

"Be sure and mention that in your eulogy."

She laughed. She had a big bawdy laugh. I liked it. A Rubens body and a Rabelaisian laugh.

"I'll have to tell Cliffie about this."

"About me being at the dealership?"

"Yeah."

"I won't be alone with that creep."

"Why?"

"Why? He was out here the other day and copped about a hundred and fifty cheap feels off me while he was 'questioning' me. God, imagine if I'd actually *cared* that the little bitch was dead, and here's some retard feeling me up. It was like being back in ninth grade. I was the first girl who had breasts and all the boys zoomed in on me."

Behind her, I saw a sleepy little girl in pajamas come into the living room, rubbing her eyes. "Mommy, I had another accident."

She leaned close and said, "Wets her bed all the time."

To her daughter: "Get in your sister's bed, then, till I'm done talking with the man here."

"But I'm *wet* too, Mommy. Cindy won't *want* me in her bed if I'm wet."

Again the whisper to me: "See what I

mean about having kids? It's always something."

A few moments later, I was back in my ragtop.

I took the ten-mile blacktop back to town. Two-lane. Less than a year old. Smooth and wrinkle-free. Just made for an Indian summer night and a car like mine. Elvis way way up singing "Mystery Train" and me with a fresh Lucky in my mouth and a sudden crazed optimism about Mary. We *were* going to find her and she *was* going to be all right and —

I saw her in the rearview.

She first appeared as headlights. Coming fast.

She was still some distance behind me, so I didn't think about it much. Lots of cars went fast. The Lord and the county supervisors had blessed us with our own drag strip — perfectly flat, a moon-silvered river running along one side, shaggy pines on the other — one of the few safe places to drag in the entire state.

Then she was less than three car lengths in back of me. Not slowing at all.

The Ford propeller-style grille. Her beautifully shaped head framed inside the driver's half of the window. Blond hair, black scarf, and dark Audrey Hepburn shades. Even at night.

All I could do was floor it. Otherwise the mystery woman would run right into me.

Then she stunned me.

She pulled out around me going eighty or eighty-five miles an hour. And man it was scary and exhilarating and wonderful and terrible all at once.

Member of the bar.

Responsible investigator for Judge Esme Anne Whitney.

Sober counselor to indigent Negroes and Indians and migrant Mexican field hands.

Former altar boy. Eagle Scout, for God's sake.

My future all ahead of me.

But right now, I didn't give a damn. I was on some kind of autopilot. Badass. Black leather jacket and motorcycle boots. Brando Dean Bogart all rolled into one.

When she pulled up alongside me and stared at me with those dark dark shades, I found myself losing control. Some *force* pressed my foot to the gas pedal, brought out my best Robert Ryan grin, made me resolve to give the mystery lady the run of her life.

We raced.

I could smell wind and river and hot car

oil. I could see an empty black slab of road and bouncing headlight patterns and diamondlike eyes of cats and raccoons hiding in the grass on the piney side of the strip.

I could hear wind and motor rev and dual exhausts and rush and roar of speed speed speed. We wouldn't make a decent can of dog food if we crashed now. She looked straight ahead. Both hands on the wheel. Roaring into the night.

Pulling ahead. Eighth of a car length. Quarter of a car length. She was going to leave me behind.

I was standing on the sonofabitch. I was yelling at the sonofabitch. I was foaming and frothing at the sonofabitch. Faster *faster.*

Crazy was what I was.

I regained some of my momentum. My hood pulled even with her rear fender. Then my hood was even with her passenger door.

I raised my ass from my seat, pushing myself against the wheel, hoping that this position would somehow add to the velocity.

I pulled up to her front fender.

Wind taste. My Lucky butt so tiny it was burning my lips. I spat it out, the flame exploding into a million minor meteorites, burning my cheek and hair. Not that I cared.

I just kept pushing, *willing*.

For the first time, she looked over at me. And then she somehow put even more power into her car.

And then I saw her. Not the mystery woman but the woman running down the piney hill to the blacktop.

She came up out of the small gully, looking crazed. She was waving her arms. Her face was smudgy with dirt and what appeared to be blood. Her blouse had been ripped so you could see her white bra and the blood smeared on her shoulder and chest. Her jeans were ripped out at the knees. She looked like an animal who has just survived a cruel ordeal.

The funny thing was, I didn't recognize her at first. I had to cut back my speed so I wouldn't run over her if she suddenly lunged onto the blacktop. That took most of my attention. The black Ford raced on ahead me, a shadow among shadows, vanishing.

My Ford bucked, swerved, screeched, whined, and bucked some more before I could fight it to a stop on the wrong side of the road. By now, the woman's image had finally registered. Mary! It was Mary!

I jumped out of the car and ran back to where she'd been.

But she wasn't there any longer.

I was alone on the blacktop. Prairie moon. Bay of coyote. Distant odor of skunk. Alone.

I ran up and down the shoulder, frantically calling her name. My legs wanted me to sit down. Bringing the ragtop from 100 mph to zero so quickly hadn't been good for me *or* the car.

I ran way past where she'd been. No sign of her.

I looked up at the pines. Had she gone back into the forest? This particular patch went on for miles. Finding her, if she had set her mind on hiding, would be impossible.

Something moved on the edge of my vision, something to the right. But when I turned to look all I saw, about three hundred feet away, was a large culvert. I could hear water trickling from it. There'd been a lot of rain recently.

She peeked out again. That's what I'd seen moments ago. She might have been a frightened deer, scared of the nearby human, uncertain of his motives.

She saw me. Our eyes met for a second. She still looked wild, bestial. And then she retreated back inside the culvert. I imagined her racing through the culvert and out the other side to the riverbank.

I had to grab her quickly.

I hurried down the gully, through the knee-high grasses, to the culvert itself. The interior smell was terrible. Rancid water, weeds, animal feces.

She crouched in the center. I could barely see her.

"I want to help you, Mary. Please don't run away."

It really *was* like talking to a frightened animal. I was afraid she'd bolt at any moment.

"Please, Mary."

I started into the culvert on hands and knees. I could feel the sodden waste soak my trousers and coat my palms. I moved inch by inch.

She starting moving too. Every time I moved, she moved. Back.

"Mary. You need help."

Our game continued. I'd move forward; she'd move backward. The stench kept getting worse.

She made her move without any warning whatsoever. She had room to turn around, and turn around she did. And immediately started scrambling from the culvert.

She was gone before I could get moving. When I crawled out to the riverbank, I saw her stumbling away far downstream. After the darkness of the culvert, the stars seemed especially low and bright and numerous.

Dark water gently lapped the bank.

I ran after her. She helped me by looking over her shoulder every few yards and by stumbling several times.

The river's edge was sand and hard mud. On a warm night like this, you'd usually find a fisherman or two. The rutted mud explained her stumbling. I stumbled a few times myself.

And then I closed on her. By this time, we were both out of breath and had slowed down measurably. I came dragging up behind her and took her shoulder and pulled her to a stop.

She screamed.

I pulled her to me and clamped my hand over her mouth.

She started kicking me in the shins. It hurt like hell.

"Mary, what's wrong with you?" I said. "It's me, McCain. McCain, Mary."

Then I saw something awful. Something impossible. Those eyes of hers. There was no recognition in them.

Exhausted, she'd quit kicking me. Quit wrestling inside my grasp. I let go of her, took my hand from her mouth.

"Mary," I said, "don't you know who I am?"

She looked at me with the frank, uncomprehending gaze of a child. In a very quiet voice, no melodrama whatsoever, she said, "I've never seen you before in my life."

PART III

Sixteen

"You're saying she has amnesia?" Miriam Travers said.

Dr. Watkins pawed at his jowly face. He still wore a black rinse on his once-gray hair and still filled his showerhead with after-shave lotion. He stank of it the way frontier docs, according to legend, had stunk of John Barleycorn. His wife had died two years ago. He was sixty-four and had just started dating. There were a lot of gentle jokes about his love life.

"Now that's one of those five-dollar words I hate to use," he said, fiddling with his stethoscope. The only hospital in Black River Falls was a sixteen-bed affair. If you were very bad off, you went to Cedar Rapids; worse than that, you went to Iowa City. He peered down at Mary, asleep in her hospital bed. She'd been cleaned up but you could still see bruises. "She's had some kind of terrible shock. So right now she's not re-membering too good."

"But she didn't even recognize *me!*" Miriam said. She'd held back tears for quite a while now. It was 2:00 A.M. and she was spent. She had a very sick husband at home and a daughter whose state had yet to be determined.

I slid my arm around her. She leaned against it, frail and weary.

"Again, Miriam, we don't know what happened. But obviously something pretty bad did. Amnesia, as they like to call it on television, comes in all kinds of forms. It rarely lasts very long. I expect in a day or two she'll be saying hello to you when you walk into the room."

"But where has she been? What happened to her?" Miriam said.

Those were the questions of the evening. I'd brought her straight to the hospital. She'd slept most of the way. Not once had she shown any recognition of me. A couple of times, I wondered if she was still alive.

"As I told you, Miriam, there's no sign of concussion. She has feeling in all her extremities. Her limbs are functioning well. And the bumps and scrapes she has are relatively minor. Cleaning them up made them look a lot less threatening. Her injuries mostly seem to be psychological. And there again, once she gets her physical strength back, she'll be better able to deal with whatever happened to her."

"Was she . . . raped?" Miriam asked,

obviously dreading the answer.

"Not that we could tell."

"I didn't tell Bill about any of this," she said to me.

"Good," I said.

"I'm not sure he could stand to hear it."

I gave her another squeeze.

"Now, I recommend some bedrest for you too. You're nearly as worn out as your daughter. You need some sleep. And you also need some help around the house."

"We can't afford it."

"I've got a high school girl who plans to go to med school at the university. She helps out in my office ten hours a week. I pay her thirty-five cents an hour. She wants to get as much experience as she can. I'll have her give you a call."

"That's very nice of you, doctor."

He smiled. "Well, isn't that what doctors are supposed to be, Miriam? Nice?"

On the way back home, she said, "She was going to tell you something."

"Yes."

"I wish I knew what it was."

"So do I."

She turned and looked at me. "I shouldn't say this, Sam. But she loves you so much."

The streets were empty. A rising wind

whipped the streetlights around, casting shifting patterns of tree leaves on the street. The cars along the curb looked like slumbering animals. All the house windows were dark.

She said, "I shouldn't have said that."

"It's fine, Miriam. It's fine. It's just I don't know what to say *back*."

She put her hand on my shoulder. "That's all right, Sam."

"I keep wondering about that envelope from the county."

"So do I. I don't know why she'd write them. What would she be looking for?"

"I'll have the Judge call over there," I said. "The woman *I* spoke to didn't want to wade back through all her correspondence. That's what she said, anyway. She was speaking to a peon so she didn't have to worry. You know how bureaucrats are. But she won't try that with the Judge."

"Judge Whitney is some woman. I wish I could be more like her in some ways."

I laughed. "Not *all* ways, huh?"

She smiled sadly. "No, I wouldn't ever want to be as stuck-up as she is. You know, you think people are stuck-up sometimes just because they're shy or because they've been hurt and they're afraid to be hurt again. But with the Judge you *know* she's stuck-up because she really does consider herself superior."

"Oh, yes. Very much. Maybe it was all the Connecticut water she drank growing up."

"Is there something wrong with Connecticut water?"

"Well, the longer you drink it," I said, "the bigger your head seems to get. There must be a connection somewhere."

The sad smile again.

When we reached her house, she leaned over and kissed me on the cheek. "You're a good man."

"Thanks, Miriam."

There were a lot of lies, social lies, I could have told just then but I didn't have the spiritual energy. You know, that everything was going to be fine. Mary would be fine. Bill would experience a miraculous recovery. And she'd open her bankbook and find an extra $100,000 in her account, the angels having deposited it before fluttering their way back to heaven.

"Good night, Miriam."

I returned her kiss. I started to get out of the car but she said, "I'm not quite that feeble yet, Sam."

I watched her walk to the door. There were a lot of people like her in our town: good, solid, hardworking people who took care of their own. Her bad luck had bent her but it hadn't beaten her. She moved slower than I'd ever seen her move before. On the porch, after getting the front door open, she turned and waved back to me.

I went home.

TV had long ago signed off. The Cedar Rapid stations never broadcast past midnight; often they went off after the eleven o'clock news. I was drained but not sleepy. I spent half an hour twisting the rabbit ears back and forth, trying to form pictures out of the noisy snow on my screen. I had a pair of rabbit ears that were the envy of Mrs. Goldman's apartment house. They must have weighed twenty pounds and had more buttons and dials and doodads and doohickeys than most intergalactic spaceships. If you knew all the right codes and combinations, it would also mow your lawn and give milk. It was quite a rig. Most nights anyway. But not tonight. Every once in a while, an image would sort of form and I'd hear dialogue and get my hopes up, but then the signal would fade and there would just be snow again. I gave up. That'd be one of the nice things about living in Chicago. You could watch TV all night.

I sat in my reading chair and drank a beer.

So many questions, including the identity of the girl in the black Ford ragtop. Would I have been in the right spot to find Mary if the mystery lady hadn't challenged me to a race? Was she some kind of guardian angel? And Mary's amnesia. The doc was probably right. Temporary amnesia was probably fairly common in accident victims. But it was still disturbing that she couldn't recognize her own mother.

I picked up a John D. MacDonald novel called *Dead Low Tide*. I'd read it a couple of times before. I always came back to it. It made me feel better in the way saying a prayer made me feel better. The ritual of repetition. There are no heroes in John D. novels, and that's probably why I like them. Every once in a while his man will behave heroically, but that still doesn't make him a hero. He has a lot of faults and he always realizes, at some point in every book, that he's flawed and less than he wants to be. I think that's why John D.'s books are so popular. Because we all know deep down we're sort of jerks. Not all the time. But every once in a while we're jerks and we have to face it and it's never fun. You see how deeply you've hurt somebody, or how you were wrong about somebody, or how you let somebody down. But facing it makes you a better person. Because maybe next time you won't be quite as petty or arrogant or cold. Good books are always moral, contrasting how we are with how we should be. And the good writer knows how to do this without ever letting on. All this is according to F. Scott Fitzgerald, as taught in lively and deft style by Dr. Harold Gelbman at the University of Iowa.

Forgive me. It was late at night and I was in a ruminative mood. Creak of old house. Jet plane far above roaring into darkness, contrail across prairie moon. Needing to take a leak but too lazy to get up. Hungry but too tired to fix anything. Sleepy now but too comfortable to walk to bed. Dozing with one cat on my lap, one cat on the arm of the chair, and one cat sleeping on the back of the chair with her head resting on the top of my head. And snoring. Cats can snore pretty good when they're up to it.

And then the phone rang.

It's a measure of how deeply asleep I was that I jumped up as if I'd been poked. The cats jumped up, too, scattered quickly.

I was baffled for a moment, staring at a small black jangling instrument I'd never seen before. I couldn't imagine what its purpose was.

And then I snatched up the receiver.

"Hello?"

Nothing.

"Hello!"

"Mr. McCain?" Very faint.

"Yes?"

"It's me. Ellie. Ellie . . . Chalmers."

"Hi, Ellie."

"I'm sorry if I woke you up."

"Just reading is all."

Silence.

"Ellie?"

"Yes."

"Is there something you want to tell me?"

"He'll be mad if I do."

"Who will?"

"My dad."

"Maybe I can help you."

"I'm just scared is all."

"What happened?"

"Sykes came to where Dad works today and hauled him out in front of everybody. They pick on him a lot anyway, on account of he was in prison."

"What happened?"

"Sat in the squad car and accused him over and over of killing the Squires woman and now Squires. A lot of the men would sneak up to the door and watch Sykes workin' him over. It hurt Dad's feelings. Now he says

Sykes is gonna arrest him for sure."

"So what's your dad going to do?"

Long silence. "Run away."

"That's the worst thing he could do."

"That's what I keep tellin' him."

"He won't get far."

"He's got money. Somebody was out here today and left a package for him."

"You know who it was?"

"Uh-uh. There was just this big manila envelope on the doorstep. Dad's name on it. There wasn't any stamp or anything."

"How do you know it was money?"

"I saw Dad open it and put it in his suitcase."

"What's supposed to happen to you, he runs off like that?"

"He said to go see you. That you're his lawyer now and you'd know what to do."

"I'm on my way out."

"I'd really appreciate it."

"You just hold him there as long as you can."

"I'll do my best."

"I appreciate the call, Ellie. You did the right thing."

"He didn't kill those people."

"I know he didn't, Ellie. I know he didn't."

Pale red fire bloomed in bursts against the dark moon-streaked sky. A war scene. It might have been night fighting in Korea.

When I reached the top of the hill looking down on Chalmers's acreage, I saw the source of the pale red bursts: two police cruisers.

Because the house was isolated from its neighbors, there were no onlookers. A cop with a shotgun stood in front of the door. I pulled up.

"He ain't gonna be happy to see *you*," Pat Jarvis said.

As far as I could tell, the only thing the Jarvis family had ever done, except butter up the priests, was produce a daughter with breasts so enormous even the withered monsignor could be seen eyeing them. Patrick had none of her charm.

"Chalmers got away, and Cliff, he figures you had somethin' to do with it."

Nice going, Mike, I thought. Give Cliffie an excuse to blow your ass off when he finally catches up with you.

"I go inside?"

"If I don't shoot you in the back, you'll know it's OK."

"Very funny."

A grin. "Ol' Cliff's pissed, and I ain't kiddin'."

I went inside. He didn't shoot me in the back.

Cliffie saw me and said, "I should plug you right here."

"There's a witness," I said, nodding to Ellie. She wore a high school sweatshirt, jeans, and white soiled sneakers without socks.

"You told him to do it, didn't you?"

He lunged at me. His face was booze red. His eyes were pretty much the same color.

"You really think I'd tell him to run? I'd lose my right to practice."

"I gave shoot-to-kill orders, in case you're interested."

Ellie started crying.

"Great, Cliffie," I said. "Why don't you scare her some more? The guy's only her father."

I sat next to her in the old high-ceiling farm living room. There'd probably been a horsehair couch in here at one time, and a Windsor chair, and a soft Victorian kerosene lamp and a Victrola. There was an overhead light on now. Bare. Merciless. The charm of the place had long ago fled.

She stopped crying and just looked scared. "He wants to kill him."

"No, he doesn't. He just likes to talk. Don't you, Chief?" I was careful not to call him Cliffie. This wasn't the time.

He glared at me. "She's old enough to understand what he done."

"He didn't do anything," I said.

"Yeah? And you can prove that?"

"Yeah, I can. I just need a few more hours."

I had no idea what I was talking about. The point was to make Ellie feel better. She sat prim and proper, sort of gangly, and more than sort of sweet.

He looked at Ellie. "Well, I hope for his sake she's more cooperative with you than she was with me. It'd be a damn sight better if Chalmers turned hisself in instead of me findin' him."

He looked around the room again, rubbed his jaw, and then left. The emergency lights died. No red-soaked bursts of illumination in the front window anymore.

I lit a Lucky.

"Can I have one?"

"Technically, I shouldn't do this, you know."

"Aw, shit, Mr. McCain, just give me one, all right? I've been smoking for years."

I gave her one. Lit it for her.

"He's probably out at the old line shack." She told me where it was.

"I thought he was going to run away."

261

"He said he wanted time to think."

"You know, Cliffie's going to put a tail on me. Everywhere I go, his tail will go. I go to the line shack, I'll lead him right to your dad."

She coughed on the cigarette.

"I thought you said you'd been smoking for years."

"Well, not steady, I didn't say. I have to smoke a couple each time before I quit coughing."

"Ah."

"He wants to kill him. Cliffie, I mean."

"He wants to kill anybody he even *suspects* is a criminal. And that means just about everybody."

"Is his old man as stupid as he is?"

"Just about."

"How'd he make all that money, then?"

I could tell she was enjoying this little respite from worrying about her father.

"Right time, right place. He had a local construction company. When the Sykeses took over, Cliffie applied for the Chief's job."

"So Old Man Sykes stepped in?"

"So Old Man Sykes appointed him." Then: "How long do you think your dad'll be at the line shack?"

"Probably all night."

"You plan on going there?"

"He told me not to."

"Then don't."

"You think Cliffie'll kill him?"

"No. I'll see to that."

"Really?" She coughed.

"Really. And meanwhile, why don't you give up the cigarettes?"

"I will if you will."

I smiled and kissed her on the forehead. "Whatever happened to respect for your elders?"

Cliffie's tail was even more amateurish than I'd expected. He followed me about half a car length back. The car was unmarked, true, but the man was in his police uniform. One sort of canceled out the other.

I was thinking about Dr. Todd Jensen. I'd been wanting to talk to him anyway. Now I wanted to talk to him as soon as possible, which meant early morning. His past with Susan Squires had always been murky. I needed to know about it in detail now, especially since he'd been identified as one of the people at Dick Keys's garage the other night.

Bed.

All three cats piled near my feet.

No trouble sleeping. Except that every

time I moved, one or two of them meowed in protest. It was OK for *them* to move, you understand, but not for me. They have that written in their contract.

I was standing outside the good doctor's door at eight o'clock, exactly fifteen minutes before his nurse arrived. She still didn't look as if she found me much of an improvement over a leper.

"He isn't in."

"I'll wait."

I sat in the reception room and went through all the boring magazines. She made coffee. She didn't offer me any. We both kept looking at the clock on the wall to her left.

I said, "If I give you a dime, can I have a cup of coffee?"

"A quarter."

"Hell, I can go down to the corner and get a cup of coffee for a dime. *Good* coffee. And a free refill."

"Then I'd suggest you go down there."

"You really don't like me, do you?"

"What was your first clue?"

"What the hell did I ever do to you?"

"I don't like your face. I hate baby faces. That's number one. And second, I hate people who get Dr. Jensen riled up. He's hard enough to deal with when he isn't riled up. But you put him in a pissy mood for two days."

"I just asked him some questions."

"That's all it took."

"How about fifteen cents?"

"How about," she said, "twenty?"

"Deal."

He came in just as I was finishing up my coffee. He wore a jaunty brown leather jacket, white shirt, necktie, chinos, and desert boots. And sunglasses. Dr. Heart-throb.

"What the hell're you doing here?" he said to me, as he picked up his phone messages.

"Looking for a few fashion tips."

"What's that supposed to mean?"

"It means we need to talk."

"Someday I'm going to punch your face in."

"I guess I don't remember that part of the Hippocratic oath."

"He's such a nuisance," his nurse said. "He got here before I did. Tried to mooch a cup of coffee."

"She charged me twenty cents. Ten cents of that belongs to you."

"Why don't you shut the hell up, McCain? I'm sick of you. What the hell're you doing here anyway?"

"Somebody saw you at the murder scene Friday night."

"Bullshit."

"I'll give you his phone number if you want."

"Should I call the police, doctor?" the nurse said.

He glared at me. "I'll talk to him."

She looked surprised. "Mrs. Malone is your first patient. She'll be here in ten minutes. You know how she hates to wait."

"Screw her," he said.

I walked through the doorway of his examining room. He reached past me and pushed the door shut. Then he took two steps back and swung at me.

All that time spent ducking the Judge's rubber hands has trained me for such a moment. I moved my head, and his hand went right into the door. Which was when, small but determined Irishman that I am, I brought up my knee. Unimaginative but effective. I got him square too.

He turned around and leaned on his examining table and started groaning, probably the way his male patients did when he gave them prostate exams.

I opened the door. "Nurse, could we have a cup of coffee in here?"

"You sonofabitch," he said.

She hurried in with the coffee. She looked at the way he was hunched over his examining table, the paper on it crinkling as his big hands bore down. "My Lord, what happened?"

"I had to perform some minor surgery. He's in recovery now."

"Doctor?" she said.

He didn't turn around and he didn't speak.

"I think he's still a little groggy from the anethestic," I said.

"Just get the hell out of here, Audrey!" he shouted over his shoulder.

"He isn't quite himself," I said, rolling my finger around my temple to indicate he was temporarily insane.

She made a ugly face at me and backed away.

This time, *I* closed the door. I started sipping the coffee she'd brought and then went to the back of the room and sat myself down where I could see his face.

"So tell me about Friday night."

"Screw you."

"You sleep with a lot of your patients, do you?"

"I don't sleep with *any* of my patients."

"You slept with Susan Squires."

"That was different."

"Oh?"

"I was in love with her."

"That why you killed her?"

He looked at me as if he were just coming out of a deep trance. "Hey."

"What?"

"I thought that coffee was for me."

"Oops. I forgot."

He was still wincing. "She always said you were a dipshit."

"Who did?"

"Susan."

"I don't believe it."

"Every time we'd see you, she'd say, 'What a little dipshit that guy is.' "

And then I did believe it because it sounded right. Some things sound right and some don't, and this one did. And I felt like hell. I'd thought we were friends, Susan and I. You can never be sure what people really think of you, I guess.

"That make you feel better?" I said.

"Damned right it did."

"You're a petty bastard."

"Yeah, well, I'd rather be a petty bastard than a dipshit."

"And they say the art of sophisticated conversation is dead."

He didn't say anything and then he said,

"I was there but I didn't kill her."

"Why were you there?"

He went over and sat down. He didn't say anything for a while. Hung his head. "We'd been seeing each other again." He was still wincing.

"Squires know?"

"I don't think so."

"And you were trying to get her to leave him?"

"Yeah. But she was pretty screwed up about the kid."

I knew what he was going to say then.

"Ellie Chalmers."

"She's Susan's kid?"

"Yeah."

"You sure?"

"Sure I'm sure. I delivered her."

"You the father?"

"She wouldn't *tell* me who the father was. That's why she left town. Everybody thought it was because she was trying to get out of the Squires thing."

"Ellie doesn't know."

He shook his head. "Fayla was her mother as far as Ellie knew. But every once in a while the whole deception bit would get to Susan and she'd drive out to the acreage and park near there with her binoculars and just look at the kid doing chores. Can you believe that shit? I felt sorry for her. Hell, I loved her. I told her if we ever got married I'd figure out some way to get Ellie to live with us."

"Chalmers knew this?"

"He knew she wasn't his kid. But he pretended she was for Fayla's sake."

"What'd Fayla get out of it?"

"Fayla and Susan went to school together. Fayla was the ugly duckling and Susan sort of adopted her. Fayla would do anything for Susan. Fayla couldn't have kids, so Ellie became her kid."

His pain erupted again. He grimaced and pushed down on his groin. "You sonofabitch."

"I don't usually do stuff like that. But when a guy your size swings on me, I don't have much choice."

"I'm gonna punch your face in someday."

"How come you didn't tell me about Ellie the first time we talked?"

He did some more writhing. He was a pretty good writher. "I didn't think it had anything to do with Susan's death. But now, with David dead, I don't know what the hell's going on. I figured you should know. If you care about Ellie as much as you seem to, I assume you'll be discreet about all this."

I stood up. Drained my coffee cup. "You

want me to get you a cup of coffee?"

"I don't want jack shit from you."

I sort of figured he'd respond that way. On my way out, I asked Audrey to take one in.

"He still could've killed her," I said.

"Dr. Jensen?"

"Uh-huh."

I ducked just in time. Judge Whitney was shooting rubber bands again.

"Then why would he have told you about Ellie?"

"Show me he was being cooperative."

"You don't think Ellie has anything to do with the murders?"

"I'm not sure."

We sat in her chambers. She wore a tailored blue suit with a stylish neck scarf. Gauloise in one hand, brandy in the other. She was forced to set one of them down when she launched her rubber bands.

"Something's bothering me," I said.

"What?"

"That's just it. I don't know. Just something gnawing at the back of my brain."

"All that cheap beer you drink."

"Oh, yeah, *I'm* a real drinker."

"Brandy, on the other hand, *clears* the mind. Gives you the most wonderful ability to concentrate."

"You sound like a commercial."

"I would be happy to endorse brandy. The right brands, of course."

I stared out the window. "It's something I know."

"Something you know?"

"Something I learned in the course of my investigation. But as yet I haven't seen its relevance. But it's there. Waving at me."

"Maybe it's making an obscene gesture." She launched another rubber band. "Very good, McCain. I've never seen you duck *under* that way before. You're getting good at this."

"What the hell could it be?" I started up from my chair.

"Don't start pacing. You drive me crazy."

"I think better when I pace."

"You're too *short* to pace. When you get behind the couch, I lose sight of you."

"Har-de-har-har."

She sighed. "I'll never understand what you see in Jackie Gleason," she said. I had used one of Gleason's signature lines. "He's so *working class.*"

"He's funny and sad at the same time," I said. "And that's not easy to be. That's what makes him such a great comic actor."

A knock.

"Yes?"

The beautiful Pamela Forrest came in. She wore a white blouse and a moderately tight black knee-length skirt. Her impossibly golden hair looked like something from myth or fairy tale. But I couldn't appreciate her this morning. Not with poor Mary in the hospital, not able to remember anything.

"You said to bring this in as soon as it came," she said, as she reached the Judge's desk. She set some papers down.

"Thank you, dear."

Pamela nodded and withdrew. She watched me carefully as she left the room. She must have noticed that I wasn't frenzied the way I usually was when she was around.

The Judge said, "Get out, McCain. I'm busy. I need to read these papers. Go home and pace or something." She'd been scanning the legal brief that Pamela brought her. She looked up. "I'd like the case solved by dinnertime tonight. I'm having a judge from the sixth district in, and I'd like to brag a little about how I uncovered the murderer."

"That would be so unlike you, Judge," I said.

A dramatic ingestion of Gauloise smoke and then the wave of a languid hand. "Now get the hell out of here. I'm busy." Then: "Oh, that envelope you wanted me to check on?"

"Yes."

"Those two initials in the corner were the initials of the clerk who sent it."

"What did they send?"

"A birth certificate."

"I'm losing my mind," Linda Granger said. "And so is Jeff. God, McCain, isn't there something you can do?"

"Well, he could always grow up."

"You know that's not going to happen."

"I'll take care of it." I told her when to be at my office. Then I called Chip O'Donlon. "Hey, Dad." And told *him* when to be at my office.

Then the phone rang.

She was crying. I couldn't understand what she said.

"Slow down, Ellie. Slow down."

"Cliffie was here. He made me tell him where my dad went. To that line shack. Then he ran out the door. There were two other cars there. Men with rifles and shotguns. They're going after him."

"Don't worry. I'll leave for the line shack right now."

By the time I got there, Cliffie had his men fanned out, encircling a weatherbeaten board shack that looked more like a large doghouse than a railroad storage shed. It

274

was up on the side of a steep autumn-blazed hill, just below a railroad track that climbed ever higher into the limestone cliffs. It was a perfect autumn day for hiking or canoeing or picking out pumpkins to carve into bogeyman faces. Butterflies and grasshoppers and leaf smoke and all that other stuff.

The men wore their hunting gear. Pheasant season didn't open for a while yet. This would be their dry run for trying out hats, caps, jackets, pants, duck calls, boots, shoes, and weapons. Lots of weapons. Enough weapons to start a small war.

Cliffie was strutting around with a .45 in one hand and a bullhorn in the other. The way some folks are good with the violin or tuba, Cliffie was good with the bullhorn.

"There's a very good chance that you can get off on an insanity charge, Mr. Chalmers!" He glanced over his shoulder and gave one of his cronies a big lurid wink. Chalmers didn't have a prayer of beating a double murder charge on an insanity plea. Not with his criminal past. "So you come out here peaceful-like and we'll drive you back to town in that brand-new patrol car of mine. It still *smells* new. You'll like that, Mr. Chalmers, I promise!"

Cliffie's police chief magazine must've run an article on how to use psychology, because usually, instead of such awkward enticements as insanity pleas and new-car smells, Cliffie would have been threatening the guy with sure death.

"There'll be a pizza tonight, Mr. Chalmers! The boys always chip in and buy a big one delivered. It's nice 'n' hot too. I'm sure they'll give you some. Our boys're nice to prisoners, despite what you might have heard to the contrary."

Cliffie had the distinction of being cited three times in six years for "the worst-run jail" in the state. Endless numbers of prisoners emerged with black eyes, broken noses, missing teeth, snapped wrists, and badly bruised ankles. As a gag, Cliffie once served up chili that he'd dumped half a pound of ground-up night crawlers in. This is one of those legends that is actually true. Everybody loves a clown.

"I'll talk to him."

He wasn't happy to see me.

"I don't believe I remember deputizing you, McCain."

"I'm his lawyer."

"You get all the important clients, huh?"

"He didn't kill anybody."

He stared at me. "She thinks she's gonna beat me this time, don't she? Show me up again?"

"This has nothing to do with Judge Whitney."

"Oh, no? She don't care if this man is guilty or not. Just as long as she makes *me* look bad. Well, I'll tell you somethin'. It ain't gonna happen this time. I got the right man, and there ain't a damned thing she can do about it."

"Then you won't mind if I go talk him into surrendering?"

He said, "Billy."

Billy Wymer instantly stepped forward, the forty-seven-year-old juvenile delinquent who does a good share of Cliffie's bidding.

"Cuff him."

"My pleasure, Chief."

"What the hell're you doing?" I said.

Wymer's a big guy with green stuff always in the corners of his dull blue eyes and a kind of moss on his stubby little teeth. His mouth is usually leaking too. When he laughs, which is frequently, especially when something cruel is taking place, he does so without sound: his mouth wide open, his mossy teeth on display, and no sound whatsoever. Like a silent movie scene.

He snapped the cuffs on me. "Got 'im, Chief."

"Good goin', Billy!" As if he'd just accomplished something major, like discovering a cancer cure or finding a new planet in the solar system. Then Cliffie smiled at me. "I tried psychology on this pecker, McCain. You heard me yerself."

"I sure did. That new-car-smell stuff would certainly have made me surrender. They could've used you when Dillinger was around."

He raised his bullhorn and aimed it at the shack. "Ninety seconds is what you got, Chalmers! You give yourself up or we open fire!"

"You can't threaten him like that," I said.

"I can't, counselor?" His eyes scanned the men. "You men get ready."

Rifles and shotguns glinted and gleamed in the fall sunlight. A lot of the men were grinning.

"This is McCain, Chalmers! Give yourself up right away!" Now that I understood Cliffie probably wasn't bluffing, it was important to haul Chalmers out of there pronto.

"Scared the shit out of you, didn't I, counselor?" Big grin on his stupid face. "Sure wish I had a photo of you just now. Sure wish I did."

"C'mon out, Chalmers!" I shouted again.

He cried back, "They'll shoot me!"

"They'll shoot you if you *don't* come out, Chalmers!"

"Forty-five seconds!" Cliffie said over the bullhorn.

"Chalmers, he'll start shooting! He really will!"

"I didn't kill those people!"

"I know you didn't. But you have to come out before I can help you!"

"Twenty-five seconds!"

"Chalmers! For God's sake! Get out of there!"

He came out. First he peeked around the door like a guilty kid. He had something in his hands.

It was sort of funny and sort of sad and sort of pathetic.

"What the hell is that?" Cliffie said.

From his fingers dangled a rosary.

"Don't shoot me, all right?"

"Tell him you won't shoot."

He raised his bullhorn again. "You men put your weapons down!"

None of them looked happy about doing so.

Chalmers came slowly down from the cabin. Arms stretched out for cuffs, black rosary beads hanging from his right hand.

When he reached me, he looked at my handcuffs and said, greatly disappointed, "How the hell you gonna help me, McCain? You're handcuffed too."

"Thanks for pointing that out," I said.

★ ★ ★

Cliffie was magnanimous and let me drive myself back to town. Sans handcuffs.

Cliffie double-parked out front so everybody'd be sure to see him bringing in Chalmers. Just in case anybody was too dense to miss all his subtle machinations, he stood in the middle of the street with his bullhorn. He wanted an audience and got one immediately: decent folk in faded housedresses and work-worn factory pants and shirts and little kids squinting into the sun to see what dangerous specimen the chief had brought in this time.

He could have pulled up behind the building, of course, and nobody would have seen him.

"Stand back, everybody," he said. "We're bringing in a desperate criminal."

Even the old ladies giggled about that one. Desperate criminal. Cliffie loved melodrama almost as much as a keynote speaker on the Fourth of July.

He repeated himself: "Stand back, everybody." Then he handed the bullhorn to Billy, yanked his own sawed-off from the front seat, opened the back door, and said, "You take it nice and easy now. You try anything, and your teeth are gonna be chewin' lead."

I hadn't heard the "chewin' lead" one

before. I hoped I didn't have to hear it ever again.

Chalmers, pale, forlorn, about as dangerous as a ground squirrel, got out of the patrol car with his head hung low. Embarrassed.

Cliffie gave him a hard shove. Chalmers turned to glare at him. Cliffie shoved him again.

I grabbed his elbow. "What's your problem?"

"He ain't movin' fast enough, counselor. *That's* my problem. Now take your hands off me." And with that he gave *me* a shove too. I knew better than to push back. He had an audience. He'd love to put on a show with me as the foil.

Inside the police station, there was a lot of noise as shoes scuffled down the narrow, dusty hallway to the interrogation room. Keys jangled. Sam Brownes creaked. Men coughed. Prisoners in the back shouted, wanting to know what was going on. The door to the cells was ajar. They wanted some kind of diversion. Cliffie wouldn't let them have radios or magazines or books.

"How about opening a window?" I said.

"I'm sorry it don't smell better for you, counselor," Cliffie said.

It smelled of sweat, puke, and tobacco. It

281

was a dingy little place not much bigger than a coffin. There was a single overhead light and a card table with a wire Webcor tape recorder on it. There were also signed black-and-white publicity stills of Norman Vincent Peale and Richard Nixon.

Cliffie pushed the still-handcuffed Chalmers in a chair and sat next to the card table. He got the recorder turned on and rolling, and said, "I'm recording every word you're going to say, Chalmers. You understand?"

Chalmers looked at me. I nodded. Then he looked at Cliffie and nodded.

It was what you might expect. Cliffie came up with twenty different ways to ask the same question which was, basically, *Why'd you kill them?* He was doing a terrible job. The County Attorney's crew would have to interrogate Chalmers themselves.

He blubbered on.

It was forty-seven minutes exactly before Cliffie needed to go to the can. I needed to talk to Chalmers.

"I'll be back," Cliffie said. "Don't you touch nothin', counselor."

We exchanged unfriendly glances and he left.

I leaned over and whispered in

Chalmers's ear, "Who sends you the check every month?"

He looked surprised and shook his head.

"It's important," I said.

"No it's not."

That's what I'd been trying to remember: the curious monthly check.

"It don't have nothin' to do with any of this." He was whispering too.

"I think it does. Ellie isn't your daughter."

"Who told you that?"

I nodded to the machine.

He whispered again, "Who told you that?"

"I figured it out. Now I need to know where your check comes from."

He looked as if he was considering telling me when Cliffie came back in.

"You didn't try 'n' erase that machine, did you?"

"Cliffie, I wouldn't try and erase the *machine*. I'd try and erase the *tape*."

"You goddamned college boys."

"Yeah, we're taking over the world."

"Shut up, now. We're going back to the questions."

Another thrilling half hour. Cliffie'd verbally lunge at Chalmers and I'd object; Cliffie'd lunge again, I'd object again. It was a dull little legal dance.

"You're gonna need a lawyer, bub."

"I got a lawyer," Chalmers said.

"I mean a real one."

"This is the comedy part of his act," I said.

A knock at the door. A cop leaned in. "The mayor says he needs to talk to you, Chief."

"He say about what?"

"He never does, Chief."

Cliffie sighed. "I finally start gettin' somewhere with this killer I got here and the mayor calls."

"Life's tough," I said, "when you're a celebrity."

"Someday I'll celebrity you, McCain," Cliffie said, standing up, which is no easy task when you weigh what he does. "And don't try and erase that" — he caught himself in time — "tape, either."

"I'm proud of you, Cliffie."

Another exchange of scowls and Cliffie was gone.

I started whispering again. "Who sends you the checks every month?"

"I don't know. They're just in my mailbox." He looked angry. "It doesn't have anything to do with these murders. You know what would happen to that kid if this town ever figured out who her real old man was?"

"Believe it or not, I think she'd like to know for herself. I think she could put up with anyone who made fun of her. And anyway, you're underestimating people here. They'd be good to her. They'd understand."

"I know a few who wouldn't."

"A few. But not many."

He sighed and started to raise his hands to wipe his face. He'd forgotten about the handcuffs. "These damned things."

"Tell me before Cliffie comes back," I whispered. "Who sends you the checks?"

Footsteps in the hall. Cliffie's steps, thunderous. Door being flung open.

And then, in that millisecond, Chalmers leaned close and told me.

Seventeen

For all the mixed reviews the Edsel had been getting, there sure were a lot of gawkers when I got over to Dick Keys's that afternoon: farmers and townspeople alike, the farmers still raw red from summer sun, the townspeople wearing the kind of tans you only get on beaches.

Three salesmen were giving the same spiel at once, each a few sentences behind the other. They sounded like a ragged chorus.

I spent a few minutes looking one over, a convertible with enough horsepower to outrun any car the highway patrol put down on the pavement. The gadgetry got me. If I ever bought a new car, I'd want a Corvette or a Thunderbird, stripped and ready for action. The interior control panel of the Edsel, with all its chrome gimmicks, was sort of comic.

"Dick around?" I asked one of the mechanics.

The guy streaked his white coverall with greasy fingers, yanked out a Cavalier, and torched a Zippo. In the middle of exhaling and coughing, he said, "He'll be right back.

He ran over to Uptown Auto to get Gil a new part." He shook his head. "Best boss I ever had, except for the Navy. He ain't afraid to pitch in, you know what I mean? Somethin' needs to be done, he don't care if he's boss or not, he'll do it."

I went in the waiting room and read an ancient *TV Guide*. There was an article on James Arness of *Gunsmoke* and how he'd played the monster in *The Thing*, and how this new guy Ernie Kovacs was ushering in a new era of "hip" TV, and then a piece on the family life of Lucy and Desi and how they really were just as lovey-dovey as they appeared on the air.

I was trying not to think about what I'd come here for.

Dick Keys was one of the town's best. He'd been around since before I was born, hawking cars and boosting the town. He was a decent guy.

He came in and said, "Rick said you were looking for me, Sam. How about you wait in my office? You want some coffee?"

"I thought maybe you'd take me for a ride."

"A ride? You serious?"

"Sure. Try out the Edsel."

He looked at me. "You? In an Edsel? C'mon. You can't shit a shitter."

"I just want to talk a little, Dick."

"Talk?"

He watched me carefully, as if I were holding something secret and suspicious behind my back.

"Yeah. Just a little talk is all."

He hesitated, then shrugged. "Talk. Sure. Why not? Well, you go pick out the beast you wanna ride in and I'll meet you on the lot."

"Appreciate it."

He started to leave the reception area and then stopped. "I heard Cliff found Chalmers."

"Yeah."

"Arrested him and charged him, huh?"

"That's the story."

"A lot of people are going to breathe easier now."

"I sure will," I said.

He smiled. "I still can't see you in an Edsel, Sam."

I picked out a lemon-and-lime one. Two-door. Not only could you make love on the seats, you could raise a family inside the plush confines of the thing.

Keys saw me and waved. He disappeared back inside, returning moments later with a pair of keys.

When he got in the driver's seat, he said,

"Believe it or not, they're starting to sell. Got a call from my buddy over in Des Moines. He said that on Saturday people acted kind've funny around them. Didn't know how to react. But he said by Sunday they started buying them. That's been my experience too. Sold three this morning, including a station wagon. Top of the line."

We were already out in traffic. Sunny Friday noon hour. We passed the library. I wanted to be sixteen again and sitting on the steps in the warmth and light and reading a science-fiction magazine — you know, the kind you have to keep the cover turned over because it always shows a half-naked girl being felt up by a purple guy with six very busy hands.

"Anyplace special?"

"How about the river road?"

"You're making me nervous, Sam." The once-handsome face had developed a slight tic under the left eye.

"I don't mean to."

"Something's going on, isn't it?"

"I guess so. Let's get out of town before we start talking."

He was wound very tight.

"How about rolling down the windows?" I said.

"Kill the a/c, you mean?"

"A/c?"

He laughed nervously. "That's car-dealer talk for air-conditioning."

"Oh. Yeah. Let's kill the a/c. The park smells great this time of year. All the leaves and everything."

"I sure wish I knew what was going on."

He killed the a/c. He had power windows. Soon we were breathing the air God intended us to.

And then we were on the river road.

The Edsel had power, no doubt about that. The river was on the right. On the left were shaggy bluffs of pin oak and pine. An old barnstormer was out for the afternoon, a real old-time showoff, swooping and tumbling and diving so fast birds sat by in frozen envy.

"Imagine how free you could be if you had a plane like that," Keys said.

"Yeah."

"I bet that's the very first thing man wished for. I mean, way back when we had just learned how to stand up straight. To fly. To have that freedom." Then he added, "To escape."

I said, gently, "Some things you can't escape, I guess."

He looked over at me. "That's what my

old man always said during the Depression. That there wasn't any escape. They went on strike, the milk farmers. Your dad ever tell you about that?"

"Uh-uh."

"Right up north of here. Hambling Road. About fifty farmers with shotguns. They were getting only a few pennies on the dollar for their milk, so they decided to make the truck drivers dump it rather than take it into the cities. They got these spiked telegraph poles and laid them across the road. Sheriff and his deputies showed up. But the men didn't back down. My uncle was one of the strikers. He always bragged about what he did. Walked right up to the sheriff with his sawed-off and said, 'I'll take your gun and your badge.' And damned if the sheriff didn't hand them over. Guess he figured my uncle would've killed him. And he probably would've, knowing Ken. So what they did was dump out half the milk and then they drove the rest on into Cedar Rapids and gave the rest away free in the poor sections. Isn't that a hell of a story?"

"Yeah," I said, and it was. "Your dad involved?"

He made a sour face. "No. Not us, me or him." He smiled with great sadness. "We're the salesman type. Talk your head off and don't *do* jack shit. Hell, half the men in this town might as well be women, the way they've lived their lives. And I'm one of them." He sighed. His knuckles were white on the steering wheel. "I haven't even taken care of my wife very well. She deserved a hell of a lot better than me. All the years she put up with me. And she didn't get anything out of it. Well, it's her turn now. I just want her to know that for once in my life I'm a man. I did something honorable. She needs to know that, and *I* need to know it too."

I wondered what he was talking about. I knew he'd killed Susan and Squires, but he wasn't exactly saying that. I needed him to say it.

"You scared to have me open this up?" he asked.

"Nah. It'd be fun."

"One hundred and twenty?"

"If it'll do it."

"Oh, it'll do it."

"Then let's go."

So we went. Faster and faster. He didn't slow down much on the long, deep curves: 90 . . . 100 . . . 105. I gripped the dash with both hands. I was starting to get cold.

He looked over at me. "Scared?"

"A little."

He looked defeated. "You figured it out, didn't you?"

One-twenty pegged. The countryside had become an impressionistic painting — colors fading one into another, the shapes of farmhouses and silos and outbuildings blurred.

"Figured what out?"

"Who killed Susan and David."

"Yeah. Yeah, I guess I did."

"This is some motor, huh?"

There were several curves ahead of us I didn't want to think about. "Yeah, it's some motor."

"Maybe I should just run us off the road."

"I don't want to die, Dick. I mean, if I've got a say in this at all."

He shook his head. "Those Rotarians aren't going to believe it, are they? When they hear who killed Susan and David." He laughed. "They're women. They sit around and gossip and bad-mouth people and then go back and sit in their offices and make their secretaries do all the work for about one-third the pay. If that."

"Just watch the road, will you?"

"It's funny, Sam. Right now I feel freer than I have since I was a boy. I really do. I feel free. I've got life and death in my hands. One little flick of the wrist and we're both dead. That's man stuff. It's not all this rah-rah business bullshit. You don't have to smile and kiss ass and be a clown all the time. I always wanted to be like my Uncle Ken. He ended up being a labor organizer. He'd bust heads when he needed to; I think he even took pleasure in it. But when I got a chance to marry the richest girl in the valley, my old man really pushed me. She couldn't even give me a child. I used to go into Chicago once a month on some pretext, and man did I whore it up. I did the whole thing: colored whores, Chinese whores, Mexican whores. You name it. While my wife was sitting home alone."

We screamed around a long curve and shot past an oncoming pickup.

When the road straightened out, he said, "You know about the kid? Ellie?"

"Yeah."

"She's a *good* kid."

"Yeah, she is."

"She doesn't know about me, and I don't ever want her to. Chalmers is an ex-con, but he's been a good father to her. I never would've believed it."

"We're coming up to Tolliver Hill, Dick. And you're on the wrong side of the road."

Tolliver Hill was a local legend. More people had been killed on it than any other hill in this part of the state. Kids drag-raced out here. The ultimate danger. One of them would end up on the wrong side of the hill as they went over it. And some poor quiet family of three or four coming up would get their grille pushed into the backseat. And everybody would be dead.

Anybody could be on the other side of that hill, I thought, as we approached it now. If he'd heard what I said, he didn't let on.

We were going far too fast for me to jump. And if I reached over for the key he might flip the car, accidentally or on purpose, it didn't matter.

For the first time, as the Edsel started up the base of the hill, the stroke of the motor sounded slightly labored.

"Get on the right side of the road!" I screamed at him.

He glanced at me. No expression. None at all. Then a grin. "Hang on, Sam. Hang on!"

We went up the hill at 106 mph, all he could get out of the car on this steep a climb. Still the wrong side of the road. Still the grin on his face. For just this moment, he was his Uncle Ken. No boring Chamber of Commerce luncheons. No more high school football booster-club meetings. No more slavish ass-kissing of old money who felt he'd married his way into respectability. He was his own man now, and a dangerous man at that. I could sense the power in his hands and arms, muscles clawing and stretching just below his skin. Certainly that power was in the madness of the sharp blue gaze and the burry rasp of the voice.

I saw the car before he did. At least, I was the one to scream first.

Coming right at us. Doing a good 70 or 80 itself.

Long drab Buick.

Wind-numb face. Heart tearing at the prison of my chest wall. Feeling five years old. Totally helpless.

Head on, it was going to be.

We were close enough now to see the Buick driver's face. Neatly combed white hair. Rimless eyeglasses. Small white hands on the steering wheel. Panic just starting to explode his facial composure.

"Keys!" I yelled. "Get over! Get over!"

He screamed.

The moment was gone. He was no longer his Uncle Ken.

He was the somewhat silly, somewhat stuffy man who always said way too much and way too little, who always told the corniest of jokes and found no setting inappropriate to selling you a car. I'd seen him whip out his deal notebook in the back of a funeral home while a wake was in progress.

He was that man again, and he was scared shitless.

He yanked the car into the proper lane. He was a good driver. He knew not to even touch the brakes. To simply put all his strength and concentration into controlling the passage of the car at this speed. His foot lifted off the accelerator. We were coasting. At around 100 mph.

Neither us of said anything. I don't think I could have. My entire body was shaking. I very badly needed to deal with my bladder. I was relieved and angry, and then — as the car began to slow significantly, as the shapes all around me fell into familiar place again — I was just relieved.

When we were at 60, he said, "I'm sorry."

I just stared out at the countryside. I wanted to spend the autumn-smoky afternoon up in the hills with the horses. Maybe take Mary up there on a picnic.

"You hear me, Sam? I said I was sorry."

"Yeah, I heard you."

"I shouldn't've done that."

"No, you shouldn't."

"I've always wanted to be reckless like that."

"Well, you made it."

We were coming into a small town named

Byrum. A Texaco station was just ahead. "I could use a pit stop."

"So could I."

He pulled into the station. It had recently been painted. You could still smell the paint. It was a friendly smell. He used the can first. I went inside and bought some Luckies.

The station man was a balding wiry guy with a pair of gleaming false teeth. "Mind if I go check out the car?" he said, as he gave me my smokes and change.

"Fine."

"Didn't get over to see one. I hear old Henry Ford'd be shittin' bricks if he ever seen a car like this one."

He went out and started inspecting it.

Keys came out of the john, which was located on the side of the station. He walked up to the front door and said, "Your turn."

"I need your keys."

"My keys?"

"Yeah."

"Why?" Then his face showed recognition. "You think I might drive off?"

"It's been known to happen."

"I could've killed us back there. And I didn't."

"I still need the keys."

"God, I don't believe this."

"The keys, Dick. Now."

"I just don't believe this!"

"Yeah, I know. You said that already."

"You think you know somebody and then look what happens. The guy don't even trust you."

"Yeah," I said. "You think you know somebody and he ends up killing two people." I lit a Lucky. Put out my hand palm up. "The keys."

He shoved his hand in his trouser pocket. I expected to see the keys. What I saw was a small .38.

The station man was back. Keys stood off and waved him inside.

"I got about twenty-three bucks in there is all, mister," he said to Keys.

"Shut up," Keys said.

"You never told me why you killed them, Dick," I said. "Why?"

He shrugged. He looked sad and scared. Panic had taken over. "He'd misspent his inheritance and needed money badly. He was my lawyer. He knew about the girl. He knew if it got out it would destroy my marriage and my career. He wanted more and more money." I noticed he used pronouns instead of specific names.

"What's he talking about?" the station man said.

"Just let him talk," I said.

"His wife was the real mother. She started sneaking out to see the girl. You know, just as a friend. I knew she'd tell her the truth someday. And my wife would find out." His tears were shocking. "All that woman wanted from me was to love her, and I couldn't do it. It just wasn't in me. I respected her and liked her and even probably cherished her in a way. But I couldn't love her and I've made her miserable. I just couldn't disgrace her too."

"You kidnapped Mary?"

"I didn't have any choice. Susan had her send off for Ellie's birth certificate — Susan didn't want her name involved — and after I killed Susan, Mary figured things out. She brought me the birth certificate and said I should turn myself in. So I grabbed her. I was going to kill her too — but I couldn't, somehow. I just couldn't."

"Give me the gun, Dick."

"Save your breath, Sam. I'm leaving."

"The gun."

I saw the station man glancing at the cash register. Probably had a small handgun of his own in there. I said, "Forget about it."

"Maybe he'll kill us."

"He won't kill us. Relax."

Keys was backing out the door. Keeping the gun on us. "Don't come after me, Sam. I need to be alone for a while. I need to figure out how to handle this."

"I'll get you the best criminal lawyer in Chicago. I promise you that. There's nothing to hide anymore, Dick. It's all coming out now anyway."

"I just need some time alone."

"Then take it."

"You won't grab this man's car and come after me?"

"Nope."

"You really won't?"

"I really won't."

"You're a good man, Sam."

"Thanks. So are you."

He looked surprised and then smiled bitterly. "Oh, yeah, that's me. Just about the nicest killer a man could hope to meet."

And then he took off running, agile for his size and age. The Edsel whipped out of the station, spewing pebbles.

The station man ran immediately to the phone on the counter and said, "Claudia, get me the sheriff's department quick."

There wasn't any way I could stop him.

301

Eighteen

"OK, McCain. Ready?"

She wanted to hear it. There was something unholy about it — her listening in on the extension phone as I informed Cliffie of the *real* killer — but one does not deny Judge Whitney her petty pleasures.

I was using the phone at Pamela's desk. The Judge was waiting to pick up in her chambers. Pamela stood in the chamber doorway, ready to signal the Judge when it was time to pick up.

I dialed. I would've taken a lot more pleasure in this if the killer had turned out to be somebody I hated. I'd been keen on David Squires being the murderer, for instance. But with Keys? I couldn't help it. I liked him. The life he'd led as a booster reminded me of the hunting scene in Sinclair Lewis's *Babbitt* where Babbitt has to take stock of his life — a very successful small-town life — and finds that none of it holds any meaning for him, that it was all a charade. And he wishes he were a little boy again and could start over; how different it would be this time. I imagined Dick Keys was going through something like that now. I imagined he was scared and lonely and remorseful, plus the fact that he'd never been able to love his wife and felt so guilty about it. . . .

"Police station."

"The Chief, please."

"Who's calling?"

"Sam McCain."

"Oh." It was not a happy *Oh*. In fact, it was a downright *un*happy *Oh*. "Hang on."

A few moments later: "Chief here."

The beautiful Pamela waving frantically for the Judge to pick up. A teeny, tiny *click* on the line.

"I just wanted to tell you, I know who the killer is, Chief."

"So do I. And he's sitting in jail right now."

"Wrong man."

"My ass."

I could imagine the rapture the Judge was experiencing.

"Dick Keys."

"Oh, sure."

"I'm serious."

"One of our leading businessmen? A deacon of my church? The man who serves hot meals to the needy every Christmas?"

"One and the same."

"I don't have time for this, McCain."

"Just listen to me." I told him everything. I gave him the name of the Texaco man who could back up my story about Keys's confession.

"But Chalmers confessed."

"If he did it's because you *beat* him into confessing."

"He fell down those stairs all by himself."

"Of course he did. Like all the others."

"What others?"

I sighed. "You've got the wrong man, Chief. I'll call the Texaco guy and have him come in and see you. He'll give you the details. In the meantime, if I were you I'd start looking for Keys."

"You bastard," he said, and slammed down the phone.

The Judge let out a most undignified yelp and came running from her chambers. She wore her judicial robes and was in her nyloned feet. She had her brandy and her Gauloise. And she threw her arms around me as if we were old lovers and planted a tasty kiss right on my lips. "Oh, God, McCain! Did you hear him!"

"I heard him."

"He's such a dunce!"

"He certainly is that."

"Beating a confession out of poor

Chalmers! The man's a Cro-Magnon!"

I noted the "poor" Chalmers. She was even feeling kindly toward the rabble at this exhilarating moment.

And then we sort of waltzed around the open expanse in front of Pamela's desk.

"Oh, I wish I had a camera!" Pamela said. "What a great picture that would make, you two dancing like that!"

"Yes," I said. "*The Judicial Quarterly* would love it for their next cover."

"You did it, McCain! You did it!"

And she gave me yet another kiss. This one, more properly, was on the cheek.

She then took a long, deep drag of her Gauloise and announced, "I shall be in my chambers. Gloating."

I couldn't help myself. I smiled. She was like a little girl on her birthday. The entire world was hers, at least for this moment.

And with that, she swept magnificently away.

"I've never seen her like this," the beautiful Pamela said. She smiled. "Guess who's taking me to the Governor's dinner Saturday night?"

"Spare me," I said.

She frowned. "I just thought you might be happy for me, McCain. I mean, we're *friends* if nothing else."

"All right. I'm happy for you."

"You don't *sound* happy."

"Inside I'm happy. Deep inside."

She looked hurt, and I realized she didn't understand that it hurt me to know she would now be spending a lot of time with Stu.

I took her hand and held it. I wanted to say something sarcastic, and then I wanted to say something genuinely, profoundly, *sickeningly* hurtful. But all I said was, quietly, "I hope you have a good time. I'm sure you'll be the most beautiful girl there."

"Thanks, McCain. I knew you had it in you."

And with that, I left.

On the way back to my office, I stopped by the hospital. The weather had changed abruptly, the way it does in Iowa. Gone the blue skies, gone the fiery trees. The sky was a cold gray, the temperature dropping quickly, already below 50 degrees. You could even smell snow. It wouldn't be long now.

Not even Fats Domino made me feel much better. I kept thinking about Keys and his poor wife. She'd be left alone. The scandal of adultery would be made far worse by the scandal of murder. In a small town like ours, murder is much more than a statistic. It brings down entire families, the way it did in the time of Balzac and Ibsen. I guess that's the understanding I get from reading. That all people are the same, no matter how far back in history you go.

I skidded into the hospital, my heel catching on the wet rubber rug at the entrance door. A nun watched me stumble head first into the lobby.

"Ed Sullivan booked me for next Sunday night, Sister," I said. "As the lead dancer."

She smiled her nun's smile and said, "She's doing much better, McCain. Much better."

"Her memory back?"

"She's started recognizing people. Most people, anyway."

A nurse was plumping Mary's pillow for her when I walked in. "There you go. A nice shower and fresh clothes, and your dinner'll be along in another hour or so."

Mary's smile was a measure of her condition. It was back to three-quarters power. Which is damned powerful, believe me.

She looked at me. There was just a moment's hesitation and then she said, "McCain!"

I walked over to her. I'd brought her a

Herman Wouk novel and flowers, which the nurse took and put in a vase. The room was an art gallery of Get Well cards and a hot-house of flower-stuffed vases.

Mary said, holding my hands, "The nurse was telling me how you found me. On the highway."

I nodded. "I owe that to the black Ford."

"The black Ford?"

I nodded. "I don't know who she is. But she's been around town lately in this Ford ragtop just like mine. Except it's black. I was out on the highway, heading into town, and she suddenly appeared. So we started to drag."

"Now, that's mature." The smile again.

"It's that clean stretch of road. You can see for a couple of miles. I couldn't help my-self. And I'm glad I did it. Dragging put me in the right spot to see you come up from that gully."

"Well, then, I take it back." She laughed. "I'm very glad you acted maturely and broke the law and endangered your life by drag-racing with a beautiful woman."

"I didn't say anything about her being beautiful."

"She'd *have* to be beautiful or the story wouldn't be as good. *All* mystery women are beautiful. It's in their club rules."

"They have club rules?"

"Oh, yes. Developed over the centuries."

"Well, then, I'd say her dues are paid up."

I leaned in and kissed her. First I kissed her on the cheek. Then I kissed her on the mouth. And I kissed her longer on the mouth than was strictly necessary.

"Say," she said. "I'll have to come to the hospital more often. I love all this attention from you. Especially the kiss."

"My pleasure." I took her hand.

She lay back. Sighed. "Sorry. I just need to rest a bit. That kiss took all my energy."

I pulled up a chair and sat down. She dozed off quickly. I didn't want to wake her up. It was all academic now anyway, what had happened to her. She was doing fine and the murderer had been caught. In time, she'd remember everything and we'd talk about it.

Dusk came early. The transition was quick. What happened was the sky darkened by four or five shades on the gray scale, letting a few stars be seen in the sweep of early night. Streetlights came on, looking lonely. You could hear news on several TV sets in other rooms. Nurses squeaked by in the hall, rubber soles official and officious. The dinner cart started rattling from room to room.

I must've held her hand for close to an hour. On and off, of course. In movies constant lovers really *are* constant. But not in life. Not in *my* life anyway. I occasionally had to take my hand back to dry off the palm, shake feeling back into it, scratch my head, light a cigarette, pour myself a little more water.

Then I'd put my hand gently back in hers and the feeling would come back. The surprising feeling of contentment, of genuine peace, that touching her had suddenly inspired in me. I put our hands on her womb, imagined a child there. And for a long time I watched the shadow play of the streetlights on her face and imagined it at various stages of her life: her thirties, her forties, her fifties, her sixties. And when she was an old woman, though it was difficult to imagine in any especially vivid away because her youth was so perfect and indelible now.

The cart came to the door. Mary woke and clipped on her light.

"You ready for dinner?" a heavy woman in a pink uniform said.

"Yes, thanks."

The smell of the food made me realize I was hungry. It also made me realize that I wasn't hungry for *hospital* food. God knows they try. You see those folks in the kitchen down there working their asses off trying their best to prepare a genuinely delicious meal. But something *happens* to hospital food. It never quite tastes familiar. It is sort of like food but not quite, the only food that can make you long for an airline meal.

She ate hungrily, fork and knife flashing. "This is great."

"First it was amnesia. Now it's delusions."

She grinned and shook her head. "Ever the cynic. This stuff is actually pretty good. Maybe I could order an extra meal for you tomorrow night."

"Only if I get to drink a quart of gin first."

"McCain, you *couldn't* drink a quart of gin. *I* can hold my liquor better than you can, and I can't hold my liquor at all."

A knock. I turned to see her mom in the door. I stood up, kissed Mary on the forehead.

"I like the way you kissed me earlier a lot better," she said.

"So did I but I don't want to shock your mother."

Her mom laughed. "Go ahead, Sam. Shock me."

I glanced at my watch. "Actually, I have to be at my office in a few minutes."

"What're you working on now?" Mary asked.

"I'd say it's a divorce case but the couple isn't actually married yet."

Mary smiled. "You're so masculine when you're incoherent."

I got the lights on, the heat up, stopped the toilet from running, started heating up yesterday's coffee, and officially retired my Captain Video notebook. It had done well by me. But now the case was officially over, it was time to salute the Captain and put him away in the bottom drawer, along with notebooks from other cases.

I spent the next half hour getting the lie-detector rig set up. I still didn't have any idea how to work it but I got it so the lights went on and the arm skittered across the rolling paper and the motor made a most impressive humming noise.

I was just finishing up when Linda and Jeff arrived. I could tell they were still estranged. They both looked awkward, afraid to even brush up against each other.

"What the hell's this all about, McCain?" Jeff asked. "I've got two very sick dogs waiting on me." Being a popular veterinarian was more than a full-time job.

"Well, there's a very sick human being you need to see too."

"Who?"

"Chip O'Donlon."

"Chip O'Donlon?"

"You two get in that closet and stay there and shut up until I tell you to come out."

"I don't like this," Linda said.

"Well, I don't especially like baby-sitting you two, either."

I was just lighting a Lucky when the knock came, a jaunty top-of-the-world-man knock. One of the rulers of the cosmos had arrived in the humble form of Chip O'Donlon. I shushed them and hurried them into the closet and closed the door. Then I went to greet my favorite narcissist.

"Hey, Dad," he said, as he walked in and gave my office his usual condescending lookover. "You got quite a pad here."

He wore a tan cashmere jacket, no less, a yellow V-neck sweater, white shirt, chocolate-colored slacks, desert boots. With his tousled hair and imposingly handsome face, he was his own Dreamboat Alert.

"I thought you didn't have any money," I said.

"I don't."

"Then where the hell'd you come up with a cashmere jacket?"

"I got friends, man." He gave me his best pretty-boy grin. "Lady friends. They buy me stuff."

The hell of it was, he was probably telling the truth.

"Sit down over there."

He glared at me. He didn't like being told what to do. "What's that?"

"Lie detector."

"You aren't putting *me* on that thing."

I had to switch tones, to the reasoning-with-an-ape voice I have to take with about a fourth of my clients. "I have to try this out on somebody I know, Chip. Just to see if it works."

"Not me."

"The Ryker job?"

"What about it?"

"Now, I know you didn't have anything to do with it."

"Damned right I didn't."

It was one of the few things Cliffie had accused him of that Chip actually didn't do. "That's the kind of question I'll be asking. Things I already know the answer to. Simple things."

He watched me suspiciously. "How come you're doing this, anyway?"

"The Judge wants me to get it rigged up before next week. She wants the District Attorney to interview a witness while the machine's running."

"I don't want to do it, man."

"I'll cancel your debt, remember?"

I'd hooked him again. That would have made me suspicious: a lawyer willing to cancel a bill — even though he knew he'd probably never be paid anyway — just to try out a lie detector set. I knew then that one town suspicion wasn't true. Chip O'Donlon *wasn't* Albert Einstein's illegitimate son.

"The whole thing?"

"Every penny."

"Wow. No more of those bullshit bills from you, man? You know it's embarrassing when the landlady sees that DEADBEAT thing next to my name on the outside of your envelopes."

"A little personal touch of mine."

He looked the machine over. "It won't give off electricity or anything?"

"Chip, it's not the electric chair. It's a lie detector. A harmless lie detector."

"Like on *Dragnet*?"

"Just like on *Dragnet*."

"It might be cool to get hooked up to it. They say if you're smart enough, you can fake it out."

I resisted the easy retort. I had to get him on my side. "I'll even take your picture, if you want me to."

"Hey!" he said. "That'd be *cool*, Dad! Strapped up to a lie detector! The chicks'll flip, man! They really will!"

A noise. In the closet.

Chip looked over. "What was that?"

"What was what?"

"That noise?"

"Oh, you must mean the mice."

"Mice? How big are they?"

"They go down to the feed mill to fill themselves up, and then they come back here to sleep."

"Man, they must really chow down."

"You wouldn't want to hear them eat, believe me. You can hear them smacking their lips for blocks."

Chip sat in the chair and looked the lie detector over, his brain, such as it was, no doubt filled with images of himself looking just like John Garfield wired to the machine. He'd probably carry autographed glossies around and hand them out at the supermarket.

"You'll really take my picture with this thing on?"

"Yeah."

"Where's your camera?"

I showed him.

"That thing work?"

"You bet."

"How old is it?"

"Not that old. Now c'mon. Let's get you hooked up."

I got the cuff on him and then sat down across from him. I'd spent a minute looking for my clipboard — a person never looks more serious and professional than when he's got a clipboard — but I couldn't find it so I had to settle for my notebook.

"Is that Captain Video?" he said.

"Yeah."

"I hate that show. Everything looks fake."

"Let's get on with it, all right?"

"Especially the robot."

"What?"

"Especially that robot, Tobor. Shit, I could build something better than that in my garage."

"Did you know that Tobor is robot spelled backward?" I figured I ought to annoy him a little more, the way he was annoying me.

"I can't believe you've got a Captain Video notebook. You don't take that thing to court, do you?"

"Not so far. Now, how about getting to work?"

"I want a cigarette in my mouth, you know, when you take the picture."

"Of course."

I got the arm working. I said, "Here we go."

"Your name?"

"You know my name."

"It's for the machine. So it'll know when you're telling the truth."

"What a stupid machine."

"Your name."

He sighed. "Chip O'Donlon."

"Age."

"Twenty-one."

And so on.

He sighed a lot, he shifted in his chair a lot, he scratched his head, his nose, his ass. He smoked and he didn't smoke. He glowered, he grimaced, he groused.

"When do we take my picture?"

"Just a few more questions."

"This is a stupid machine."

"Yes, I believe you've made that point several times." Then I said, "Now, so far, you've told the truth."

An arrogant smile only the Chip O'Donlons of the world can offer us. "Or maybe I beat the machine."

"I'm glad you said that."

"You are?"

"Yeah. Because I think a guy of your intelligence — I think that's just what you've done. I think you answered falsely a couple of times. But I don't think the machine got it."

He beamed, he preened.

"So I'm going to ask you just two more questions."

The smirk. "I'm ready, Daddy-o. Any time you are."

I looked at my notebook as if Moses himself had left a message for me to read. "The Harrison Auto Parts store robbery last March. You have anything to do with that?"

It stopped him, as I hoped it would. The eyes narrowed; the teeth lost some of their gleam; the jaw muscles started to bunch.

"How'd you know about that?"

"It's just a question I made up is all."

"Yeah, well, I don't know shit about it."

I looked over at the arm of the detector. "You're good, O'Donlon. You're very good."

He looked down at the arm too. Looked up. The smirk was back. He was under the impression he'd beaten the machine again.

"All right, one final question."

"When do we take my picture?"

"Right after this question."

"I want time to comb my hair."

"Don't worry."

He glared at the machine. "This thing's a joke. A moron could beat this thing."

Yes, I thought uncharitably, and a moron just has.

"All right. Here's the big question. You ready?"

"God, you make it sound like *The $64,000 Question* or something."

I studied my notebook again and raised my eyes slowly. "Have you ever slept with Linda Granger?"

"What the hell kinda question is that?"

"It just popped into my mind. And you've been *telling* everybody you have. So I thought I'd just ask."

"Of course I did. *She* came to *me*. Spent the whole night at my apartment."

"Then you actually made love to her?"

"I actually made love to her. The same way I do to all the broads. What's so special about her? She's nobody, believe me. Nobody. And the jerk she goes with. What a loser!"

I half expected Jeff to come piling out of the closet, but there was silence.

And then the arm on the machine started to move. The fact that I nudged the machine with my knee may have had something to do with it.

"Look," I said.

He looked down.

The arm was still bouncing all over the page. The markings were violent, wild strokes.

"What the hell's that mean?"

"It means you were lying and it caught you."

"Bullshit I was lying."

"It means you've been going all over town telling people you slept with her when you didn't."

"The hell if I *didn't* sleep with her."

"Well, the machine says otherwise."

"The machine is stupid."

Now I played outraged prosecutor. I jumped up and went over to him as he started to get up. I shoved him back into his chair.

"You're lying, aren't you?"

"What the hell are you gettin' so hopped up about?" He looked intimidated. Pretty, he might be; tough, he wasn't.

"Because you shouldn't say things that aren't the truth."

"She's nobody. Who gives a shit?"

I walked to the desk. Pointed to the phone. "You know who I'm going to call?"

"Who?"

"Cliff Sykes."

"The police chief?"

"Yeah."

"For what?"

"To tell him about the Harrison Auto Parts robbery."

"Tell him what?"

"That you were the one who did it."

"Bullshit I did it."

"Bullshit you didn't. Frankie Hayes told me all about it. He's a client of mine and he tells me everything."

"That little prick."

"So you tell me the truth about Linda Granger or I call Cliffie and tell him what you and Frankie did. Frankie's underage. They'll try him as a juvenile. But for you this could be real bad. First time you do a serious crime, and you screw it up and get caught."

He slouched back insolently in his chair and sighed. "All right, so I didn't screw her. So what?"

"But you've been *telling* people you screwed her."

"So I exaggerated a little. Big deal. Every guy exaggerates."

I sat on the edge of my desk, like Perry Mason does on Saturday night. "What happened that night?"

The deep sigh again. "Some bare tit. A little dry humping. And then she was crying and wailing about how much she missed Jeff and how she'd only come over to make him jealous. Then she puked all over my couch and I threw her in my bed so she could sleep it off. Bitch slept till practically eleven the next morning. She didn't even help me clean up the couch. Said she was too hung over and in too much trouble with her folks."

"Bare tit and a little dry humping and that was it?"

"That was it." Then: "Frankie really told you about the Harrison job?"

I shook my head. "No, but it sure sounded like you two. I just took my best guess."

Then the closet door burst open.

Jeff went right over to O'Donlon. "You ruined her reputation with a lie, you bastard!"

"What the hell were you doin' in the closet?"

Then Linda came out. She too went for O'Donlon and slapped him hard across the face. "That's for calling me a nobody!"

I could see Jeff was about to swing on him so I stepped between them.

"I want t'take him outside."

"Forget it, Jeff. You got what you want."

Linda put her arm through his. Pulled him away from O'Donlon. "Thanks, McCain."

"My pleasure."

"I really owe you one," Jeff said.

"I didn't even get my picture taken," O'Donlon said.

I made O'Donlon leave first.

While they waited, Jeff said, "I'm sorry, Linda. I would've married you anyway. I really would've."

He said it magnanimously, which was a mistake.

"Don't do me any favors," she said.

He looked at me, then back at her. "I love

you, Linda. And I want to marry you." This time it came from the heart.

And then they were kissing and I was trying not to pay any attention.

When I said good-bye to them I planned to go home, open a can of Falstaff, pick up a paperback, and relax. I'd earned a good rest and I planned to take it.

Nineteen

I was just locking the door when I heard a car sweep up behind me in the two-car parking space. A voice behind me said, "Hold it right there, counselor."

Cliffie.

I came down the stairs. Turned my collar up. There was a mist that would soon be rain. Cold drops of it pattered in the leaves. The air smelled fresh and clean. There was an odd, quiet excitement about the first true night of fall. Time to haul out my bunny jammies with the feet in them. I already had a Captain Video notebook, why the hell not go all the way?

"You hear the news?" he asked. He'd left his motor running, lights on. He was silhouetted in the beams. The motor, which needed a tune-up, throbbed. I smelled car oil and gasoline.

"What news?"

He shook his head. "The sumbitch did it, all right."

"I'm not following you."

"Keys. You said he did it and he did. Judge Whitney is probably sitting out in her mansion right now, gloating."

Which she probably was, in fact.

"You interrogate him?"

"Not hardly," he said. "Nobody'll be puttin' that head back together. Not even the funeral-home fellas."

"What're you talking about?"

"He blew his damned head off is what I'm talkin' about."

"When was this?"

"One of my men found him about an hour ago. In the park. Down near the boat dock. He'd put a gun in his mouth. I seen it myself. A stinkin' mess is what it is."

"Oh, God."

"What's that for? He killed them people, didn't he? Even left a note *sayin'* he did."

"He was a decent guy."

"Yeah, McCain. Most decent guys I know go around killin' people."

"So he's in the morgue?"

"Yeah. Novotny's comin' over after supper to do the autopsy." He laughed. "Way that sumbitch eats, might be tomorrow by the time he gets there."

I felt empty. "Guess I'll go home."

"I just wanted to warn you about next time."

"Next time?"

"Yeah, next time there's a murder. I catch

you interferin' with the investigation again, counselor, I'm gonna throw your ass in jail. Get me?"

"Yeah." I was too drained to argue. "Got it."

"And remember it."

"I'll remember."

"And tell the Judge. I'll throw her ass in jail too."

I could just see Judge Whitney in a cell, running the jail staff into exhaustion with her orders.

He got in the car and drove off.

I couldn't help it. I felt sorry for Keys. What Cliffie said was indisputably true. Good men don't go around murdering people. But sometimes bad people are good people too. Or good people can do bad things. Life is like that sometimes.

I took a shortcut home, passing Dick Keys's car dealership. Life went on. Even on a misty night like this one, people were out looking at the new and used cars. The Edsel was still drawing crowds.

When I saw two of the three service doors open and lights inside, I remembered the spare tire. I really needed to change it.

I wheeled up to one of the open doors and went inside. Only a couple of men were working. A radio was on. Guy Mitchell was "Singing the Blues." So were we all, pal. Only two of the bays were being used. A large wrench fell to the floor, the clang unnaturally loud.

Henry had his head up under a monster-size Packard of ancient vintage.

"Hi, Henry."

He brought his head out where I could see it. "Hey, McCain. You hear about Dick?"

"Yeah."

Shook his dark head. "Poor bastard." Then, "Wonder what the missus'll do. Way she depended on him and all."

"Yeah," I said. "I was wondering about that myself."

He glanced at the big clock on the wall. "If I want to get home to a warm meal, I got to get back to work here."

"I just stopped to pick up my tire."

"Oh, yeah. Right. I'll go get it for you."

He broke into a half run. His mention of a warm meal sounded good. He was back in two minutes. "Here you go." He rolled it to me. "I ain't got the form or anything. You can just stop in tomorrow and pay at the service desk. Just a buck is all. That's the sixth flat I've had to fix because of that damned taillight. Hell, even Mrs. Keys got a flat. It's back there, too, all ready to go. Well, got to get back at it." I did remember the mechanic taking a flat tire out of her car trunk the day after the murder, once Henry mentioned it.

I thanked him and left. Pitched the tire in the trunk. Fired up the Ford and headed home.

And about two blocks from my place I remembered something Mrs. Keys had told me: that she'd been helping decorate the showroom until about seven-thirty on the night Susan was killed but had then gone home and stayed there for the rest of the night. If that were the case, how had she managed to get a flat tire from the taillight? Amy Squires hadn't had her accident at the dealership that night until two hours later.

The Tudor was dark except for a faint light in a distant room on the ground floor. In the whipping wind and heavy mist, the house looked like a fortress of civilization standing bravely against the chaos of the darkness.

I pulled up to the garage and went up to the front door. I'd forgotten how heavy the shield-shaped knocker was. It pounded twice against the night.

She didn't come for several minutes, but I could hear somebody moving around so I waited for her. She was in shadow so deep I couldn't see anything but a faint shape when the door was finally opened. "Hello, Sam."

"Hi, Mrs. Keys. I just wanted to tell you how sorry I am."

"I had to take the phone off the hook. Everyone calling to wish me well and tell me how much they loved him." Her voice trembled with tears.

"I feel the same way. He was a good man."

"He certainly was."

I snapped my fingers. "Say, I was just down at the garage and they told me to tell you your tire is ready."

"Oh. Yes. The tire. I'd forgotten about it."

"Seems you ran over that taillight too."

"Yes, I guess I must have." She was on autopilot. Not thinking of what she was saying.

"And that's kinda funny, you know."

"What is, Sam?"

"That you ran over that taillight before seven-thirty sometime."

"I guess I'm not following you."

"Didn't you tell me the other day that you were down at the dealership till seven-thirty and then you came home for the rest of the night?"

"Gosh, Sam, if you say so."

"Well, I talked to the woman who broke

the taillight, and she didn't *have* the accident until around nine-thirty. You see what I'm saying, Mrs. Keys?"

Hesitation. Now she was fully engaged. No more autopilot. Cautious. "No. No, I guess I don't, Sam."

"It's just that it would've been hard to get a flat tire when the accident hadn't even happened yet."

"And you're saying what exactly?"

I still couldn't see her. She was a night being, a disembodied voice.

"I don't know what I'm saying exactly, Mrs. Keys. I thought maybe you could help me."

"I'd like you to leave. I don't think I like you anymore, Sam."

"He felt so guilty about you, Mrs. Keys, that you know what I think?"

"I don't care what you think." She started to shut the door.

I had to say it fast. "I think you murdered those two people and he covered for you. I think it was the only way he felt he could pay you back for your lives together. He really felt terrible about not loving you, Mrs. Keys."

The longest silence I could ever remember. The door stopped halfway open. Then: "He really said that to you? About feeling terrible?"

"He said it several times, in fact."

"I loved him so much, Sam."

"I know."

"And when David Squires threatened to tell everybody about the daughter Dick and Susan Squires had. . . . All I had left was my dignity, Sam." She was just then starting to cry, but it was a hard, dry sound. I suspected she'd been crying most of the day and there wasn't much left. "I didn't want to end my life in scandal. People always said he married me for my money. And I suspect he did. But he always made sure I had my dignity. He ran around, but he did it out of town and he never told anybody. I really appreciated that. I really did. And I believe he respected me too."

"He did."

"And genuinely liked me."

"He liked you very much."

"Maybe if I could've given him children —"

I eased open the screen door and took her in my arms. She found a lot more tears than I would've thought possible.

I put her on the couch and found a winter coat in the front closet to use as a blanket and then went to the bar and poured us both a Scotch.

My first impulse was to call the Judge and tell her what had happened. But I couldn't do it. Mrs. Keys needed a good night's rest.

"Took a lot of strength to get Susan in the trunk and drag Squires out of the cable car," I said.

She said, "I was always strong for my size — athletic." Then: "Do we have to go right away?"

"Not right away."

"Are you hungry?"

"Actually, yes, I am."

"I make a mean breakfast. Not lunch or dinner, but breakfast. How does that sound?"

"Sounds good."

I sat in the big fashionable kitchen watching her make bacon, eggs, and hash browns. The scents were seductive as hell.

And as she cooked, she talked. "He took much better care of me than he thought, Sam. He didn't love me but he respected me and he kept me from being hurt. I know how plain I am. But he was always telling me how attractive I looked." She glanced at me and smiled. "He even had *me* half believing it. He was a very good talker, as you know."

I set the table in the breakfast nook. She brought over the food and I brought over the coffee. We sat down and ate.

"I'm not scared," she said, after we'd

forked through our food for a while. "I know I probably should be."

"You're a good risk for bail. You won't be in jail long."

She looked over at me, and I was reminded again of a Roman sculpture. Dick hadn't been just flattering her. She really *was* an attractive woman. Much more attractive the older she got.

"I'll be spending the rest of my life in prison, won't I?"

"I really can't say."

"But if you had to bet —"

I shrugged. "I'm not much for betting, I guess."

"How's the food?"

"Great."

"I'm going to give Chalmers and Ellie a lot of money."

"They're good people."

"Yes. As unlikely as it seems, he is in fact a good man. And she's a great kid. Dick loved her very much."

"Yeah, I think he did."

I poured us some more coffee.

"Would you like to be my lawyer?"

I smiled. "That's very nice of you. But you need a hotshot."

"Do you know any hotshots?"

"A good one in Cedar Rapids."

"Would you be willing to call him before you call Cliffie?"

"I really need to call him *after* I call Cliffie. To keep things kosher with the law, I mean."

She had a nice, weary smile. "Then that's what we'll do, isn't it?" Then: "I'm sorry I killed them, you know. I mean, I'm not really a heartless beast."

"Gee, really? You had *me* fooled. I figured you for a heartless beast for sure."

"They were going to destroy us, Dick and me."

"There had to be a better way, Mrs. Keys."

She was silent.

I looked at her for a long time and said very quietly, "Maybe now I should call Cliffie."

She looked back at me, and for a moment there I thought she might start crying but she didn't. "Yes," she said. "Maybe now would be a good time to call him, wouldn't it?"

Twenty

Mary was in the hospital another week, by which time she remembered just about everything, including the sad — but still spooky — sight of Dick Keys trying to work himself up to killing her in the cold cabin where he'd kept her. Once she went home we spent several evenings playing cards and watching TV together. I was so grateful she was alive and getting well, I didn't think about Pamela Forrest much, which was good news for everybody. One night, when we were sure her folks were asleep, we really got into some randy sex on the couch in front of the TV. We knew we didn't dare risk going all the way there, but we had a lot of fun anyway. It was like being back in high school again and how could you beat that?

Jeff and Linda got married. Chip O'Donlon got the crap beat out of him by a jealous husband. And the Judge, over the Thanksgiving weekend, flew to New York, where she was a dinner guest at Lenny Bernstein's place. At Christmastime, one of our sidewalk Santas got arrested for being intoxicated, Old Lady Arness emptied a shotgun into the Nash Rambler belonging to an IRS man who was trying to collect back revenues, and our basketball team came within three points of beating the number-one ranked team in the state.

And then one day I got a perfumed envelope, out of which dropped a wallet-sized color photo of the gorgeous mystery lady: the blond hair, the black head scarf, the black shades, the black Ford.

On the back it said: *We'll meet again someday, McCain.*

I sat there and stared at it for a long, long time.

And then I took out my billfold and slipped the photo into one of the plastic windows. Right between the photos of Mary Travers and Pamela Forrest.

I was a blessed man. I was, a truly blessed man.

The employees of Thorndike Press hope you have enjoyed this Large Print book. All our Large Print titles are designed for easy reading, and all our books are made to last. Other Thorndike Press Large Print books are available at your library, through selected bookstores, or directly from us.

For information about titles, please call:

(800) 223-1244
(800) 223-6121

To share your comments, please write:

Publisher
Thorndike Press
P.O. Box 159
Thorndike, Maine 04986

#311